Danger
Follows

Danger Follows

Goerky Smith

JOURNEY BOOKS™

Greenville, South Carolina

Library of Congress Cataloging-in-Publication Data

Smith, Goerky 1947-
    Danger Follows / Goerky Smith.
       p.   cm.
    Summary: While exploring nesting sites for turtles in the South
Pacific, Jill and her parents rely on God's protection when they
realize that their sailboat has been bugged and they are being
followed.
    ISBN 1-57924-070-4
    [1. Adventure and adventurers—Fiction.   2. Oceania—Fiction.
3. Christian life—Fiction.]   I. Title
PZ7.S6486Dan   1998
[Fic]—dc21   98-42385
                                              CIP
                                              AC

Danger Follows

Edited by Debbie L. Parker
Designed by Duane A. Nichols
Cover by Rich Cutter

© 1998 Bob Jones University Press
Greenville, South Carolina 29614

ISBN 1-57924-070-4

15   14   13   12   11   10 9 8 7 6 5 4 3 2 1

For my parents:

Betty Kirkhart Goerky,
a living epistle of God's love

and Charles M. Goerky,
whose faith moved mountains

with special thanks to M. Susanne Smith
and Gertrude Patton Little

Contents

Down Under

CHAPTER 01

No smoking and *fasten seatbelt* signs flashed as the airliner prepared for a midnight departure from Honolulu. A woman's voice explained emergency procedures. Jill Wyman had heard the same tape on their departure from Miami, and then at Houston and San Francisco, so this time she tuned it out.

The jet engines began to build power, vibrating the plane. The cabin lights dimmed, and Jill was thrust back in her seat as the white runway lights flashed by. In seconds, the lights of Honolulu lay below like glitter on black velvet. When the seatbelt signs blinked off, Jill yawned to relieve the pressure in her ears.

Random thoughts circled through her tired brain. Her aquariums at home . . . Sure was nice of Grandma to take care of the fish . . . Wonder how Chip is doing. I miss her! But she's such a bouncy dog, she'd probably bounce right off the sailboat.

She yawned again. Her parents, sitting next to her, were already dozing. Tomorrow is going to be a big day, she told herself. Better get some sleep. She shut off the cold flow of air from the vent and closed her eyes.

After several long, fitful hours, morning came. Jill munched a ham bagel while she gazed at the blue ocean, thousands of feet below. Sailing the South Pacific will be great, she thought, but I wish we could spend more than a few hours in Australia. Not just to see Steve, of course. The pictures he sent looked interesting—especially the Outback.

Jill nudged her father. "The Great Barrier Reef."

DANGER FOLLOWS

Far to her right, the dark blue ocean was spotted with islands. Between them lay brilliant blue lagoons, the color of the turquoise earrings she had received for her fourteenth birthday.

He leaned over to peer out the window. "If the pilot hadn't changed course to avoid a storm, we would have missed it. See how the water over the shallow reef is lighter than the deeper water?" Smile lines softened his steel-gray eyes.

Jill's mother, seated near the aisle, looked up over her reading glasses. "It's more than a thousand miles long," she said. "Rick, we really should come back when we're not on a schedule. I've always wanted to dive here. The Reef has the world's best variety of underwater plant and animal life."

"You could have made that your postdoctoral research project instead of turtles, Anne," he replied. "I could have played golf and watched Australian Rules football instead of driving around the South Pacific looking for—what? Pearls? Pirate treasure? Sunken ships? Real estate?" He grinned. "No, nothing sensible that will make me a wealthy man. We're looking for safe homes for turtles."

"My turtles," Jill said, "always preferred condos with a Jacuzzi."

Jill's mother laughed and took off her glasses. "So, this is how the trip is going to be. Here I was, thanking God that I have my family with me on a business trip, and you both gang up on me! Mutiny, and we're not even at sea!"

Jill smiled and returned to her thoughts about Steve and sailing. But soon the jet dropped its nose slightly and started its approach to the international airport at Sydney. At the sight of tall office buildings and a broad expanse of red-tiled roofs, she snapped back to the present. The *fasten seatbelt* light flashed.

I hope Steve remembered to ask his father to meet our plane, she thought.

"Ladies and gentlemen," the captain said, "we are now approaching the international airport at Sydney. Welcome to Australia from our crew and from TransPacific. G'day!"

As soon as they'd checked through immigration, Jill spotted Steve's red hair in the tightly pressed crowd. She was startled by the changes in his appearance. His face was leaner, more like a man's. And he was taller.

Guess I've changed some too, she thought shyly.

Surprise registered in Steve's eyes, then a smile lit his sun-flushed, freckled face.

The tanned, wiry man standing next to Steve extended his hand. "Great to see you again, Rick."

"Wade! Good of you to meet our plane."

"We expect a payback. We're counting on you staying with us tonight. Not many friends from the States fly in, you know." He took the hand Jill's mother offered. "Will that fit in with your plans, Anne?"

"It's kind of you," she replied. "We could all use a good night's sleep."

After they retrieved their luggage, they piled into a station wagon driven by Steve's father. "We'll drop you off at the shipyard so you can check on your sailboat," Mr. James said. "Steve and I have some errands to run."

"Jill, I have tickets for a football game this afternoon," Steve said. "Want to go with us?"

She flashed him a smile. "Sure. What's the fun of being in Australia if you can't see kangaroos or a football game?"

Sea birds wheeled and cried over the harbor, which looked as congested as downtown Sydney. Boats of all sizes crowded the bay, and the marinas looked like thick forests of rigging and masts. Mr. James drove along the harbor and finally turned into a parking lot beside a small shipyard.

As soon as Jill stepped out of the car, the sun's full intensity hit, and she wished she'd worn something lighter. She would have given a week's allowance for a cold soda, but her mother had only one thing in mind—the sailboat.

They crossed the parking lot to a plank walkway that led to a small building. A sign hung above the door. She could barely make out the weather-faded lettering: *T. Bligh's Shipyard.*

The gray planks, a hollow echo beneath their feet, were sand-encrusted. Grass grew in crevices between the boards, and the edges were decayed.

She saw her parents exchange a look, and it made her feel uneasy.

Her mother paused, looking over the rundown property. "It's been more than ten years since I was here. This used to be a small but neatly run business. I should have supervised the commissioning of our sailboat myself." She sighed and squared her shoulders as if determined to make the best of it.

Inside the office, a thin, bald-headed man sat at a cluttered desk. A cigarette, propped on the edge of a tar-blackened clamshell, fogged the room.

"Close the door. Close it, I say! Can't stand the smell of fish," he rasped, coughing. "Whole ocean smells like fish. Fish, fish, fish."

Jill closed the door reluctantly, shutting out the fresh sea breeze. The man shuffled some papers, then squinted at them, one eyebrow raised in irritation. "We don't do tours anymore. Ferries and harbor cruises leave from Circular Quay. Can't help you." He bent his head over a large ledger.

Her father leaned over the desk. Resting the knuckles of his large hands on the desk, he looked the man straight in the eye. "We're looking for Chandler Björnson. I understand he works here. Where can we find him?"

Whether it was her father's six-foot-two stature or the chandler's name that caused the bookkeeper's reaction, she couldn't tell, but he stuttered nervously as he gave them directions.

Jill's parents exchanged another glance, then silently left the office and stepped onto the crumbling boardwalk. She closed the door and hurried after them.

Old Friends

CHAPTER 02

Jill was the first to spot the *Sailfish*, moored to the pier. Before she could point it out, three men emerged from the sailboat's cabin. One, a stocky man wearing the Bligh's Shipyard logo, was arguing with the other two.

A silver-haired man in a business suit smiled at him and threw a brown envelope on the deck. At that moment, the third man, dressed like a sailor, turned and stared coldly at Jill. He was big and blond. Muscular. With ice-blue eyes.

A shark, Jill thought. That look in his eyes—like a shark's.

The man in the suit spoke to the shark-eyed man, and they left the *Sailfish* together.

"Dad?" she asked.

"I saw it, too, Jill, but I don't know what to make of it."

The stocky man bent to pick up the envelope and slipped it inside his jacket. Then he pulled out a pipe, lit it, and coolly surveyed Jill and her parents as they approached. Finally, a smile spread across his broad face.

"You must be the Wymans," he said. "Björnson here. Hope you find the *Sailfish* to your satisfaction."

Jill's worry gave way to pleasure as she explored the boat.

Freshly painted, the forty-two-foot sailboat had plenty of room for three people. It had a powerful diesel auxiliary engine and an up-to-date satellite navigation system.

The well-stocked galley boasted a propane stove and a large propane-fueled fridge. Real food, she thought, starting to get hungry. I can cook real food like hotdogs and nachos. She peeked into her cabin, aft on the starboard side, opposite her mother's laboratory.

Björnson followed them around the boat and seemed happy that his work was appreciated. He nodded approval while her mother wrote a draft on her expense account to pay him.

"Well, we at Bligh's Shipyard aims to please. Now, would you like to see the nuts and bolts of how things work around here?"

Bligh's Shipyard. What an odd name, she thought, remembering the sign over the office.

"Missus Wyman, here are the systems manuals—"

"Mr. Björnson, who is T. Bligh?" asked Jill.

"Not now," her mother said. "We need to hear what he has to say."

"That's all right, ma'am," Björnson said. "All this here,"—he waved his pipe at the shipyard—"is his'n—Captain Bligh's." He turned away from them, puffing on his pipe and mumbling under his breath. "Not that he would get his hands dirty working here, mind you."

"Sir?" Jill asked, hoping he would repeat what he'd said.

"You might have seen him earlier—the fine-looking man in the fine suit. Now, where were we? Oh, yes. Now when you measure the fuel level in the tanks . . ."

After pointing out key features, Björnson said, "Mr. Wyman, I've stowed those charts you wanted with details of islands and your ports of call. And there's info on weather and a current *Nautical Almanac*. I trust you have a sextant in case all this mumbo-jumbo satellite navigation goes on the blink during a solar flare?"

Her father smiled. "Sure do."

"Well, you better. Wouldn't be surprised if'n all them satellites fell out of the sky one night like shootin' stars. Any sailor bears that in mind." Björnson exhaled a sharp puff of smoke.

Steve's father returned two hours later and helped stow the luggage onboard. Then he and Steve took Jill to the promised football game.

Australian Rules! To Jill, it looked like a mix of football, rugby, and soccer—a rough free-for-all. Two teams clashed on a field with four goal posts, kicking and throwing the ball to score. The crowd went wild with enthusiasm.

Steve's team lost by a narrow margin, so his father treated them to three-layer sundaes as consolation.

"Sounds like you've got state-of-the-art equipment on that boat," Steve said. "If you need another crew member, be sure to fax me."

"Very gallant, Steve." Jill remembered the envy of her friends when they heard she would sun, sail, and swim while they waited every day for the school bell to ring.

Steve's dark eyes reflected the same interest she'd seen in them earlier, and she spooned another bite of ice cream, pretending not to notice.

"How did you manage to skip school?" asked Mr. James.

"Really, I'm not on vacation." She smiled, trying to focus on the question, not Steve's eyes. "I have homework, book reports, stuff like that. When I get back, I have to turn in notebooks and pass exams."

"Sounds like school," Steve admitted.

As they drove through traffic toward the outskirts of the city, Steve chatted about what had happened since he'd moved to Australia. Jill wondered about the puppy—one of Chip's—that she'd given him.

"How's Microchip?"

"He's no runt, now," Steve said.

Mr. James smiled. "If you ask me—or if you don't—he's more of a turbocharged dust mop."

"There's a resemblance," Steve conceded.

Jill looked over at Steve and his father. She could see a good bit of resemblance there, too, except for Steve's auburn hair. They both had even features, broad shoulders, a good sense of humor. And, she thought, feeling her face flush, Steve is sort of cute—for an old friend, that is.

"Remember how Micro looked when I got him?"

She nodded. His short fuzzy hair stuck up all over. He was the scrawniest pup in Chip's litter, but he was the only pup Steve wanted. She'd been happy to see the ball of fur tucked under her best friend's arm, even when it meant the pup would end up in Australia.

"Does he still eat Limburger cheese?"

Steve held his nose. "And barbecue chips and pizza with anchovies. Anything that won't bite him first. The dog has no taste."

"Well, I brought Micro some Limburger."

"No wonder you smell so funny."

"Give it up, Steve!" she said, wondering how she could ever have thought he was cute. "Oh, no! I left the cheese with my bags on the *Sailfish*."

"Which will have to be aired out for six months before you can leave port," he said, laughing. "It will be the only boat easier smelled than seen."

They pulled into the driveway of a two-story frame house, and a medium-sized bundle of shaggy gray hair streaked out to the car. As soon as Jill opened the door, it bounded into the front seat.

"Looks like Chip, but bigger." She laughed as she struggled to calm the wriggling, silver-haired dog.

"Micro, remember Jill?" Steve tried unsuccessfully to hold the dog still.

If the mop-haired dog didn't remember, she couldn't tell by the greeting. Micro offered his paw, barked, and covered her face with puppy kisses. Jill gave him a hug and followed Mr. James inside.

She had just dropped her bag in the guest room when Steve knocked at the door. "Put your stuff up, and come see my collection."

He keeps his room neater than I do, Jill thought, remembering how she had pushed papers and socks out of sight before leaving. At one end of the room were shelves lined with books and sports equipment. Above a desk on the other end was a colorful collection of curved, flat sticks. Some were painted with animals and geometric designs.

"Boomerangs, aren't they?" she asked.

Steve took two off the wall.

"Do they come back when you throw them?"

"No, not all of them. This kind does." He held up a light, L-shaped stick. "Australian natives, the Aborigines, used these to scrape, dig, and hunt." He pointed to a larger stick, just slightly curved. "That won't come back when you throw it. It was used for hunting and fighting."

"Great collection. Where'd you get them?"

"Here and there. I made some."

"How do you throw them?"

"Come on; I'll show you." Steve chose two boomerangs, one light, the other heavy, and led her outside.

She eyed Steve's grip on the curved stick as he drew back his arm and released it. The boomerang whipped through the air and arced back toward Steve. He caught it easily and handed it to her.

After several tries, she found she could catch the smoothly polished piece of wood if she pretended it was a tennis ball and kept her eye on it.

They took turns throwing until she accidentally hit Steve and he crumpled, pretending to be hurt. "Aaugh! Fire a warning shot!" he yelled.

"Don't catch with your knees!" she said.

He picked up the heavy hunting boomerang. "Now, this one you don't want to catch."

After he set up a row of tin cans, he used the stick to knock them down. Then he tossed a can and hit it in midair. He retrieved the boomerang, blew imaginary smoke off one end, and shoved it into his belt.

"Fastest down under," he said, swaggering like a gunslinger.

Jill laughed as he clowned. Later they played tennis until daylight faded. It was like old times.

"Miss you on the tennis team," she said, collapsing on the back steps.

Steve laughed. "You mean you miss beating me."

Condos for Turtles

CHAPTER 03

"How did you get into this turtle project?" Steve asked, as the two families attacked steaks, salad, and baked potatoes.

"Mom's been working on it for about four years now," Jill said.

Her mother spoke up. "The project funding came at the same time as Rick's Navy retirement plans—an answer to prayer! Otherwise, I'd have had to work with a hired crew."

"And I'd be stuck in a classroom," Jill said.

"Anne, what exactly is it you're looking for?" Mr. James pushed his chair back from the table. "Jill says you're building condos for homeless turtles?"

Jill's father smiled. "Yes, sir! That's what she's doing."

Her mother shook her head and smiled at them both. "I study the plants and animals living in the ocean, especially sea turtles."

Steve's eyes lit with interest. "Mysterious, aren't they? Some travel thousands of miles to reach their nesting sites."

"Yes, they do, Steve, but they're being pushed out of some of their major nesting sites by pollution and poaching. And traffic! Have you ever seen hundreds of hatchlings crushed on a highway?"

"No," he said, "but I've read about it. And talk about poaching! First time I ever saw a sea turtle, it was big, about three hundred pounds. Wasted. A hunter stripped a few pounds of meat from the bottom shell and threw the rest on the beach."

Steve seems really interested, Jill thought. Turtles are so . . . so *slow*. So green. So boring. She picked at a paper napkin, shredding it as she thought about the *Sailfish*. Tomorrow morning—we'll be on our way.

"Are you looking for nesting sites, Anne?" Mr. James asked.

"Well, most of the major nesting sites are identified. I'm interested in whether sea turtles can be tricked into changing their nesting sites. We're looking for isolated areas with good conditions for transplanting turtle eggs and hatchlings."

After the dishes were cleared away, the talk turned to the nitty-gritty of the Wymans' trip. Charts were laid on the table, and Jill noticed that Steve shared her interest in ocean currents, weather, and ports of call.

Makes sense, she thought, since his dad is a pilot and a weekend sailor.

She listened closely to Mr. James's advice, but when the conversation turned from the sea to funding and government approval, she lost interest. She and Steve slipped back to the den to use the ham radio. They spent the rest of the evening there, finally contacting Jill's cousins who lived on a ranch on the other side of Australia.

The next morning she woke to the aroma of frying bacon and glanced at the clock. Oh, no! Quickly she showered, dressed, and brushed her wet hair into a ponytail.

Minutes later, she stuffed her nightshirt and brush into her bag, then followed her nose to the kitchen. Steve was stacking buttered toast on a table already spread with eggs, bacon, and blueberry muffins.

"Good morning, Jill." Mr. James handed her a cup of black coffee. "Good to see you join the living. When you didn't hear that alarm shake your room this morning, Steve was going to call the medics!"

Jill smiled sleepily. "Breakfast smells wonderful." She stirred milk and sugar into the coffee. And more sugar. And more milk. Then she ate with relish, listening as the adults talked.

Was it her imagination, or did Mr. James sound concerned about their trip?

"Well, you picked the best time of the year," he said finally. "You do plan to be back before hurricane season?"

Her mother laughed and stood up to clear the table. "Yes, we sure do." She turned to Jill. "Bag packed? It's time."

"Coming." Jill ran back to grab her toothbrush, then she impulsively pulled a can of new tennis balls from her bag and tossed it to Steve.

"It was fun," she said. "Like old times."

He grinned. Then he chose a boomerang from his collection and handed it to her. "You can practice with this," he said.

She looked at the heavy boomerang curiously. It was painted with a large emu and small kangaroos. "Practice on a sailboat? No way, but thanks. This will look great in my room."

The sun was just rising as they reached the harbor. The smells of salt water, fish, and diesel oil were heavy in the air. The morning breeze and the waves lapping gently against the pier made Jill eager to set sail.

The two families paused on the dock, and Steve said a simple prayer, asking God's protection on Jill and her parents. One at a time, they swung onto the deck, and Mr. James handed them their bags.

"Thank you," Jill said. "Thanks for everything."

"Give us a call when you're back in port. Keep your eyes open. It's a big ocean out there!" Mr. James saluted, then he and Steve turned toward their car.

After Jill stowed their bags, she loosened the mooring line. The engine, under her father's deft touch, coughed, then purred like a happy tiger.

As they eased through the harbor, flocks of sea birds wheeled overhead. They slipped past the Sydney Opera House, then under the Harbour Bridge and through Port Jackson.

Halyards creaked, and sails climbed masts as Jill followed her mother's orders. The shoreline receded, and buildings and boats grew smaller and smaller until they looked like toy models.

The sails bulged, fat, full, and dazzling white. Sunlight glinted off the ocean like gold coins. Jill gazed at the blue sailfish that flew above the deck. She lifted her chin and let the salty breeze whip through her hair. "Well, *Sailfish*," she whispered, "we're off!"

Something Fishy

With the coastline far behind, Jill and her parents worked steadily to become familiar with the *Sailfish*. As the wind shifted and blew diagonally against them, they hurried to adjust the sails.

She was as happy as she was busy. Unknown to her parents, she had read about sailing for months before they left, making sketches and memorizing nautical vocabulary.

The last few weeks of school had dragged unbearably. She'd found herself drawing sailboats on English papers, labeling main and mizzen masts instead of nouns and verbs, and defining *outhauls* and *larboard strakes* instead of *formidable* and *osteoporosis*.

Fortunately, two of her teachers had seized the only slant that held her attention. Her history teacher had asked her to draw a time line to show the importance of American naval power during the War of 1812. Her English teacher told her to report on the conflict between good and evil in a Herman Melville book about whaling. She'd tackled the projects with enthusiasm.

Her first day on the *Sailfish* passed into late afternoon by the time she realized she was seasick. Oh, no! she thought. Something you've anticipated for a year couldn't possibly make you sick. She fought the nausea that swept over her.

"Jill?" Her mother looked at her with concern.

"Nothing, Mom. Really, nothing." But she couldn't say it like she meant it.

"Seasick?"

"Me? No way. Not me." Then she ran to the stern of the sailboat and leaned over the rail.

Her mother shook her head sympathetically. She followed Jill down the steps to the galley, then handed her a cold drink and a wet cloth to put on her forehead.

"Maybe you're just hungry. It's six o'clock. You've worked all day with nothing to eat since breakfast."

She gave her a few crackers which, amazingly, tasted good, then held up a can of chicken noodle soup. "Not great for our first meal at sea, but we can put the Tacos Supreme on tomorrow's menu."

A little later Jill stretched out on her bunk to close her eyes for a few minutes. As she slept, she dreamed she was attacked by fierce-faced, tattooed pirates. Knives between their teeth, they rode turtles—nine-hundred-pound, man-eating sea turtles.

As one of the giant turtles was about to bite, her eyes popped open, and she sat upright, clutching her pillow. She felt the forward movement of the *Sailfish* and stared around the cabin, trying to get her bearings.

Then she remembered. She was at sea! She stretched, instantly wide awake. Every muscle in her body ached, but the nausea she'd felt the night before was gone.

She dangled her legs over the side of the bunk gingerly, afraid that sudden movement would bring back the seasickness, but her stomach, other than being empty, was calm, and her head felt clear.

She left her cabin, walked through the main living area, and paused in the galley. It's a miniature kitchen, she thought, like in a child's playhouse.

A screech came from her parents' cabin. "Yee-ick!" Her mother charged through the main cabin, holding her nose. With the other hand, she held a shirt as far out as her arm would stretch. She scrambled up the companionway to the deck.

A strong odor filled Jill's nostrils. Something rotten . . . like Limburger cheese. And that, she realized, pinching her nose, was just what it was.

Before they'd left the States, she had carefully wrapped a piece of the aged cheese in plastic. Because of the potent smell, she'd double-bagged it before stuffing it into her canvas bag. She'd hoped the treat would help Microchip remember her. Too bad she'd left it onboard the *Sailfish* when they visited Steve's family.

"Jill?" Her mother held the shirt with one hand and her nose with the other.

"Sorry! I forgot about it."

"You packed Limburger cheese in your bag!" her mother said. "This is a new way to make nachos or something? You have a hidden hunger? A nutritional deprivation?" With her nose pinched, Mom sounded like a cartoon character with a head cold.

As sorry as she was for smelling up the cabin, Jill couldn't help laughing. Still holding her nose, she carried the bag on deck and found the offending chunk of cheese. She threw it overboard. "Whew! Let's make some fish happy."

They rinsed out her clothes in the cockpit, using a hand-held shower hose, and Jill thought about that cheese. "Mom, something's fishy." She hung the last T-shirt on the lifeline that was stretched along the deck.

"Cheesy, not fishy," her mother said.

"No, I mean it, really. I double-wrapped that cheese and put it in the manicure kit Aunt Diane gave me. You know, all wrapped so the smell couldn't get out. I wouldn't do anything dumb like throw a piece of cheese in the middle of a clothes bag."

"Hum. Are you saying that my snorkeling, tennis-playing teen hasn't slowed down long enough to open her manicure kit and polish her nails?"

She smiled at her mother's description. "No, but I will—sometime when I get bored." Then she remembered. After they'd left the harbor, something just hadn't felt right when she'd stepped into the main cabin. She had shrugged the feeling off, however, since everything seemed to be in order.

Mumbling something about the air pollution index, her mother went below to fix breakfast. Jill sat down in the cockpit beside her father. He lounged with one hand on the large wheel, the other holding a mug of black coffee.

For a moment Jill gazed ahead of them at the vast expanse of rolling blue waves. "Dad, did you notice anything unusual yesterday?"

"About what, Jill?"

"I don't know. Anything unusual about your papers or bags. Anything."

"No," he said, sipping his coffee. "Of course, I make it a point to keep our vital documents with me."

She frowned, wondering if she should say anything.

"Thinking about those men on the dock?"

"Maybe. I'm not sure. Really, it sounds dumb, but I think maybe someone went through our bags."

As soon as she said it, Jill shook her head. "No, I guess not. Maybe I didn't pack carefully. Or probably things got messed up when our luggage was tossed around."

Her father was silent for a minute. "Well, remember—*In every thing by prayer and supplication with thanksgiving . . .* "

"I know, *let your requests be made known unto God.* But don't you think this is too stupid to pray about?"

"Actually, I pray about everything. Besides, your concern isn't stupid."

Just then her mother stepped onto the deck, an aroma of fried ham clinging to the towel she had tied around her waist.

"Rick, why don't you take a break and eat something hot," she said. "Jill and I can handle everything."

"Food?" He asked, raising an eyebrow in feigned disbelief. "Real food?"

"Uh-huh. Ham, biscuits, orange juice, the works."

"Umm. Real biscuits? From scratch? Like Mom used to make?"

"Real biscuits from a box like Mom used to make," she said, swatting him with the towel. "And if you don't leave now, I'm going to withdraw my generous offer. Oh, and bring us plates when you're through eating. And juice. And I want my coffee hot with two creams and—"

"Sure, if there's any left." He ducked the towel she threw at him and disappeared into the cabin.

Later that afternoon, Jill was sitting on deck, enjoying the steady breeze and the rhythm of the *Sailfish* when she saw a large, oval body roll on the surface. It reflected sunlight like a gigantic silver coin.

As their boat drew closer, the strange creature jumped out of the water, then vanished, smacking the waves like a belly-slamming high diver.

"*Mola mola,*" her mother said. She shaded her eyes, squinting at the spot where the odd fish had disappeared.

"It's a funny name for a fish."

"It's a funny fish for a fish," her mother said. "*Mola mola*—headfish—a slimy fish that likes to sunbathe and eat jellyfish. He won't hurt you, unless his looks scare you to death."

"It was huge," Jill said. "It slammed into the water like it weighed a ton."

"Could have. You may use my library to check it out."

That evening, she chose a book about tropical fish. Maybe she'd find something about the what's-its-name. *Mola mola.* Hmm. Two tons!

Well, she thought, thumbing through the pages, learning is fun—sometimes.

The next morning she had to remind herself of that opinion. Actually, today was her first day of real study. After getting used to the *Sailfish*, she and her parents had set a schedule, rotating duties so that Jill could keep up with her schoolwork.

She settled herself on deck with a book. For inspiration, she glanced at the words Dad had scribbled in her notebook. *If your mother and I hadn't done homework, Jill, we wouldn't be here now. God expects you to develop the talents He has given you.*

She had just started reading when she heard the faint buzz of a plane. It didn't sound like a large jet . . . more like a small private plane, the type chartered for business trips between islands. She watched idly as the plane passed the boat, then circled back at a lower altitude as though someone wanted to take a closer look.

Suddenly, the plane swooped toward them, growing larger and larger, its engines roaring ominously. Jill clutched at her book and leaned back.

"What does that idiot think he's doing!" her father exclaimed.

The plane dived, like a hawk attacking its prey.

At the last second, it pulled up. Then it veered right, heading northeast.

Jill jumped to her feet. "He barely missed the mainsail!"

She hung over the rail, staring after it. A few inches closer and both the plane and the *Sailfish* would have been matchsticks. What had Mr. James said? *Keep your eyes open! It's a big ocean out there.*

She could tell her parents were shaken but didn't want to worry her. She noticed, however, that her father logged the incident, along with the time, coordinates, and the number written on the side of the plane.

Too distracted to study, she sprawled on deck, watching the ocean. She didn't even feel like eating the warm peanut butter and carob cookies her mother had baked. Soon she closed her eyes, lulled by the warm sun and cool breeze. Half-asleep, she heard her mother say, "You have a good background for handling emergencies."

Maybe she means Dad's Navy experience, Jill thought. She tried to remember everything she knew about her dad's military work, but it wasn't much. She'd accidentally discovered that he used to work with important government secrets. Something had gone wrong. People—who weren't supposed to know—found out who he was. After that, they had moved closer to Mom's parents. Later, her father had switched jobs, then retired from the Navy. That's not much to know about your own father's work, she thought sleepily.

The last thing she remembered before dozing off was her mother's reassuring comment. "Nothing to do with you, Rick. Probably a pilot misusing drugs or showing off."

By the time she awoke an hour later, Jill could see the faint outline of land in the distance. Her appetite was back, and the cookies quickly vanished from the plate.

While she helped her father take in the sails and switch to auxiliary power, her mother guided the *Sailfish* into a busy anchorage along the southwest shore of New Caledonia. It was still well before noon when they eased into a bay filled with sailboats, motorboats, and yachts, cutting their speed to a turtle's pace to avoid rocking a small catamaran with a red and white sail.

After refueling the boat and slipping into shore clothes, they locked the cabin and went ashore. Jill's father carried his briefcase firmly under one arm.

How strange it felt to walk on something that wasn't moving under her feet!

They caught a blue minibus headed for the *Place des Cocotiers*, and Jill sat next to a window. "Nouméa—Paris of the Pacific!" her mother said, her voice tinged with excitement. "First stop, the heart of Nouméa, the town square."

"Mom," Jill whispered, "you sound like a travel brochure."

Nouméa was a mix of old and new: stately old colonial buildings, glass and concrete offices, small shops, and modern department stores. Her mother pointed out a garden wall draped with purple bougainvillea blossoms and a courtyard bright with red poinsettias and pink hibiscus.

The traffic was heavy for midmorning. So noisy. What would it be like during the morning rush hour?

They got off the bus at the square, a park with tall trees, fountains, and statues, and Jill paid the driver with coins Steve's father had given her. As they stopped by a tourist office on the bustling *Rue Anatole France*, she wished again that they were on vacation, not business. She studied the city map, then looked innocently at her mother.

"It would be easy to get lost here. The streets all have the same name—*Rue*."

"You show serious symptoms of becoming a tease like your father," her mother said, "because I know that you know *rue* means street."

In good spirits, they followed their street map, stopping first at a bank to exchange a traveler's check for local currency, then at a small curio shop filled with shells, beads, and post cards.

On a table cluttered with polished shells, Jill found a four-inch laciniated conch. She rubbed the smooth purple mouth. The scalloped edges are lovely, she thought. It would look great in my collection, but I'd rather find shells on the beach. She put the conch back and bought a post card.

After her mother found a hat that she jauntily wore for the rest of their time ashore, they walked to the post office.

From his briefcase, her father pulled a special envelope for mailing undeveloped film, along with two official-looking letters. She wondered if her dad's letters had anything to do with that crazy pilot.

She scribbled a brief note to her grandparents. *The ocean is beautiful. I miss you. Thanks for taking care of Chip and my fish. Hope Chip doesn't drive you crazy!*

Near the post office, they found a small restaurant with red-and-white-checked tablecloths. At last, food! Jill stared at the menu, then she laid it on the table. "This isn't English. How do they expect me to know what I want if I can't read it?"

"Yep, looks like French to me," her father said. "Hum. I suppose you would like the *champignons provencales* and *escargots au vin?*"

"What's that?"

"Mushrooms with garlic and parsley. And snails in wine sauce."

"Sounds too expensive. I don't want to hurt your budget."

"That's very considerate of you. Well, then, how about a hamburger and French fries?"

"Yes!"

"Mr. Wyman, my budget's not *that* tight," her mother said. "What about the baby lagoon scallops seasoned with garlic and parsley?"

Although the dock was within walking distance, they caught the bus back because their arms were loaded with bags of fresh fruits and vegetables; warm, crusty loaves of French bread; and Valmeuse cheese.

"So, can I make nachos with Valmeuse?" Jill asked.

"Fine," her mother said, "but not with my share!"

After getting off the bus, they strolled to the dock where they had moored the *Sailfish*. Not far from their boat, Jill passed a muscular seaman who looked familiar. Where had she seen him before?

As she looked at him more closely, the man stepped into a bead-curtained shop, but she had seen enough. He wasn't dressed like a sailor anymore. Now he wore a sleeveless black shirt and jeans.

Her mouth felt dry and her hands, cold.

He was the blond man she had seen at Bligh's Shipyard. With the shark-eyes. What was he doing here?

Questions

Harbor waters lapping against the dock were gray, reflecting overcast skies, as the *Sailfish* slipped away from the port of Nouméa the next morning.

They passed heavy barges, commercial fishing ships, and freighters moving slowly out to sea. Jill's father set a course northeast for the Fiji Islands.

That afternoon, she sat in the captain's seat, guiding the spirited *Sailfish* which was under full sail to catch every wisp of breeze. It was her favorite job, but all afternoon the face of the shark-eyed man haunted her.

The wind blowing on her face, dolphins playing in the waves—nothing dimmed the image of the sailor's face. Nothing silenced the question in her mind. What was that blond man doing in Nouméa?

She absently greeted her mother and relinquished the helm. I'm sure that man is following us, she thought. Why? She stepped out of the bright sunlight and down into the cabin.

Her father finished a calculation, then swiveled his chair around. "Smooth operation this afternoon. You have a good feel for sailing."

Pleased that he had noticed, she smiled. She had felt more confident today. Watching gauges and manning controls was getting easier. Maybe that's why she'd had more time to think . . . and more time to worry.

She took an orange soda from the fridge and slipped into the booth. Should she tell him or not?

Her father sipped his coffee, then gestured toward the screens behind him. "Ready to bite off radar reading, radiotelephone frequencies, and satellite navigation?"

"Sure," she said. "I mean, *no. Yes.* What I mean is, sure, I'm reading the manuals, but there's something I can't figure."

Here it goes, she thought. I have to say something.

"And?" He put down his mug and pushed back his chair.

"Dad, I'm almost positive I—no, I've thought about it, and I'm sure. I saw one of the men who was with Björnson the morning we picked up the *Sailfish*."

"Where?" He crossed his arms, listening.

"He was on the dock in New Caledonia." She spoke slowly, trying to picture the man accurately. "He was tall and strong-looking. Blond. Very muscular. Kind of bald on top, but his hair was long in back. At first, I thought I was seeing things, but now I'm sure. It was the same man."

"So now you're adding two and two, and the sum is more than four?"

"Something like that. And, I've been watching you. You don't feel right about things either. After that pilot tried to land on a forty-two-foot runway, I heard you and Mom talking."

For a moment, she thought she saw alarm flash in her father's eyes. He cleared his throat. "Jill, there's information we haven't shared with you for your own protection. And there's information I can't share with you or your mother."

"I understand that, but these instant replays go through my head. The envelope that man threw at Björnson. The wrapped cheese that unwrapped. That crazy pilot. And now I see someone in New Caledonia who's supposed to be in Australia. So, am I imagining things or what?"

"Well," her father said thoughtfully, "it's not unusual for a ship's chandler to have an argument. His expenses for outfitting a ship could have run high. Maybe the owner thought it was too high. And how many times was our luggage handled? Bags are thrown onto conveyor belts and jostled in transit."

True, she thought, but that cheese was double-bagged.

"As for the air-affair, somewhere every day I'm sure some drug abuser or infantile showoff—like that pilot—foolishly risks his life."

She shifted uneasily and stared at her soda. Does Dad think I'm jumping to conclusions? I've tried not to do that.

"Now, as far as your observation goes—that I'm uneasy about what's happening . . ." He leaned forward in his chair. "You're absolutely correct. There's no solid proof, but I believe your suspicions are valid."

"What?"

"I share your reservations. Also, I've made contact with an old Navy buddy to see if something is going on in this area that I'm not aware of. Especially if it is something that involves us. I don't know anything yet."

He patted Jill's hand. "I'll tell you if I uncover anything that concerns us. I promise you that."

"So—so what do we do now?"

"I've made the necessary contacts, so now we wait."

"Wait!"

"Let me amend that. We wait, we pray, and we keep our eyes open."

"Does Mom know?" Somehow Jill wanted to protect her mother from worrying.

"She knows we're trusting God and keeping our eyes open, but she's used to that. You don't glue transmitters to twenty-pound Biminis lobsters or chase packs of three-foot barracudas around the Red Sea if you can't keep your eyes open."

"Mom's done stuff like that?"

"She slowed a little when she started changing your diapers."

"Dad," she objected, embarrassed, "not to change the subject, but what can I do?"

"Well, after we stop in the Fiji Islands, we'll change our schedule. In the meantime, let's work on your education."

"Schoolwork?" How could he think about lessons during such a serious talk?

"Navigation and maintenance. I want you as confident with every aspect of running the *Sailfish* as I am."

Normally, she would have been flattered, but she sensed the urgency in her father's voice. She determined that she wouldn't let him down.

Over the next few days, it rained off and on, but fortunately, the showers weren't accompanied by high winds or large ocean swells. On deck, Jill learned to watch the ocean for unexpected hazards: large pieces of driftwood, oil drums, submerged reefs, anything that could endanger a small sailboat a thousand miles from land.

Below deck, she found another world that intrigued her. She used the satellite navigation monitor, studying the digital readouts beamed from space with their location. As the wind and seas altered their heading, she made course adjustments.

Too bad I can't be graded in this, she thought.

One morning, a brilliant white sea bird with a black mask perched on the fiberglass radome over the radar antenna. High above the deck, he looked down at Jill and her parents as they ate breakfast in the cockpit. "A booby!" she whispered.

After a few minutes, the bird flew from its perch to sit on the molded seat that circled the cockpit well. Cautiously, he eyed a small plate of toast.

Delighted, Jill tore off a piece of bread, gently tossing it in front of the sea bird. It fluttered its black-trimmed wings, watching her with bright eyes, then snatched the bread.

Maybe I can make a pet out of him, she thought, as it flew back to its perch. Throughout the day, she enticed it with bits of dried bread and crackers.

She discovered that the sociable bird shared her love of nachos (no cheese and peppers). "What should I name you?" she asked, as the sea bird took another chip from her outstretched hand.

"I could call you Bandit because you wear a mask. Or Piglet because you eat like a pig. Or Speedy because you fly so fast. Hum. I know. Turbo. You look like an incoming missile when you dive for fish. So, Turbo it is."

For the next few days, Turbo stayed near the sailboat, and she was grateful for his company. It made her realize how much she missed Chip.

Early one morning the cries of sea birds awakened her. There must be a thousand of them out there, she thought. She jumped from her bunk, threw on her clothes, and leaped up the steps.

A cloud of sea birds circled overhead, as if inviting the *Sailfish* with its white, wind-filled wings, to join them. Then, like wind-blown snowflakes, they rose and headed toward the open sea. Turbo flew with them.

"Birds of a feather," her mother quipped.

"Yep, a handout's not everything," her father said from the captain's seat.

With a sense of loss, Jill watched the flock until it disappeared. If only . . . , she thought. If only I had a friend here with me, someone my own age. It would be so much fun. Or if I could have brought Chip. Why did I think this would be so great?

"Well, Jill, I'm sorry, but it looks like your feathered friend is gone," her mother said.

She stared at the deck without answering, then went below to her cabin. She picked up a book, sighed, and stretched across the berth. Finally loneliness faded, and she studied until she heard the cry, "Land ho!"

She rushed on deck, excited to see the faint blur of the Fiji Islands becoming more distinct on the horizon.

The *Sailfish* eased into Suva with Jill at the helm. Her father stood on the forward deck, and her mother sat beside him, hands clasped around her knees.

They docked, and Jill checked the fuel level in all five tanks. After they'd refueled, she walked around with a clipboard noting the number of gallons pumped into the tanks.

Puzzled, she looked at the record, checking it again.

She checked the reading a third time, then walked aft to talk with her father. "We've been cheated! We were shorted about seventy-five gallons in Nouméa. The gauges all read full at the time, but I didn't check. I didn't plumb the tanks through the filler necks. We didn't use that much fuel. I logged the running time on the engine."

He nodded agreement, looking at the daily log in which he had just made an entry.

"You're right. We've been running on sail most of the time. Did you record the gallonage pumped into each individual tank to fill it?"

"Uh-huh, I set the counter back to zero every time we changed the fill from one tank to another."

"Could be the gauge in one or more of the tanks was sticking," he said thoughtfully. "Or the shortage could have been an over-sight—but I don't think so. Especially not when Björnson asked such detailed questions about our ports of destination. I think he wanted to know where to find us."

"Then you don't think the fuel shortage is a mistake?"

"No, I don't. Our 'friends,' whoever they are, are staying in touch. If we had needed that fuel, we would be stranded right now."

And in danger, Jill thought.

"Should we call it off?" her mother asked. "Our lives are more important than this study. If someone is trying to sabotage our—"

"Anne, I don't know what's going on, but canceling this study probably won't cancel the problem. Jill, go with your mother to get supplies. Many of the shop owners speak English as well as Fijian, so you can get what we need. I'll fill the potable water and liquid petroleum tanks and keep an eye on things. We'll leave when you return."

Jill's mind raced with questions, but she nodded.

As she stepped onto the dock, her glance fell on a man who stood on the deck of a chartered fishing boat nearby. His back was turned to her, but she noticed that he wore a wet suit, and he was strapping on some diving gear. Then he slipped into the water carrying an odd-shaped parcel.

Midnight Attack

CHAPTER 06

Sailing northeast, Jill's father followed an altered course toward a cluster of coral islands. Her mother had chosen the islands because they were uninhabited and away from heavily trafficked shipping lanes.

Jill and her parents did not leave the helm or radar unmanned except for short breaks and for meals, or mess, as her father called it, which they ate together, weather permitting. Although they used the autopilot and radar at night, they took turns on deck watch.

After Jill's discovery of the fuel shortage, her father spent more time keeping the boat in top condition and watching for any sign of trouble. When freighters or small oceangoing vessels popped up on radar, he monitored them until they blipped off the screen, moving away from the *Sailfish*.

Often on night watch, when the *Sailfish* threw a frail path of light on the black ocean, she saw her father in the cockpit, reading his Bible by flashlight. The sight reassured her, and she tried not to worry.

One morning, instead of studying, she fished while the boat idled and her father made a repair. But that afternoon, she made herself get back on schedule. Book propped on one knee, she lounged in the dining booth eating nachos and trying to untangle the events of World War II.

She yawned. Afternoons were the worst times to study! Her mind wandered to Steve and the fun they'd had. She got up to find an orange soda and dragged her thoughts back to school.

What would I teach if I were in charge? Science? Yes. It's interesting. Math? Of course. Even Captain Bligh made the midshipmen on the HMS *Bounty* study math. English? No way. But write-ups are part of science. Well, maybe. History? Never. Anything that's dead—and history is dead—should be buried.

Still trying to stay awake, she threw cold water on her face, then opened her book again.

She studied about World War II from the German invasion of Poland to the war at sea. She'd just read about the battleship *Bismarck* when her father called, "Land ho!"

She flung her book onto the table and took the companionway in two steps.

When she reached the deck, an island was in plain view, and her father was taking depth readings. They approached from the northwest toward a cove that offered protected anchorage.

Their first stop was a tropical paradise. Morning glories fringed a white sandy beach, and tall palm trees swayed gently in the breeze. To Jill's right was a thick tangle of red mangrove trees, dropping their secondary trunks like long-legged spiders. To her left rose the island's central peak.

Near the cove, a stiff breeze caught their boat. Jill was so busy that she didn't look at the island again until they dropped anchor.

While she packed supplies, she overheard her father send a terse radio message. At first, she thought she hadn't heard the transmission correctly, then she realized it was a code.

"Jesse's son headed for Saul's hometown, but he went to Elah Valley instead. Track this boy. Will he see a nine-foot Philistine?"

Just as she strained to hear more, her mother asked her to help load the dinghy. One thing she knew for sure, their quiet passage had not lessened her father's concern.

"Madame," her father said, as the three beached their small craft, "I move that all business be adjourned until your crew has been fed. If you continue to withhold our rations of salt beef and grog, you will have a mutiny on your hands. Or a crew too puny to work."

"Hear! Hear!" Jill said.

"It's been moved and seconded that we eat. All in favor!" her mother said. She handed a bag of sandwiches to Jill. "Rick, please ask the blessing."

They ate lunch in silence, gazing around the small cove. Then her mother asked, "So, Jill, how are your studies coming? Are you keeping up with your work?"

"I'm a chapter ahead in science. Electricity, measuring current and resistance, that kind of thing. The next unit's better—planets and constellations."

"And your other studies?"

Jill took a bite of her sandwich. "A little behind in history. Everything else is okay."

Her mother raised an eyebrow. "Hmm. Think you can catch up?"

"Yes." Jill sighed. "Later tonight."

"Good." Her mother held up the Thermos. "More iced tea anyone?"

After eating, Jill helped take sand and water samples. While her mother logged descriptions of plant and animal life, she excused herself to look around. Parallel lines of whitecaps broke over the shoreline. A sea bird flew so close she could have reached out and touched its belly.

For a time she stood still, soaking up the wild quietness of it all, then she walked into the water. The warm-cool waves splashed over her, pulling the sand from under her feet. How quickly the sand disappeared! She remembered the story Jesus had told about the two house builders. One man had built on rock, the other on sand.

She sat on the beach and molded handfuls of wet sand into a lopsided castle and moat. But by the time she'd finished the tiny turrets, the incoming tide started to wash away the walls.

What had Jesus said about building on sand? *And every one that heareth these sayings of mine, and doeth them not, shall be likened unto a foolish man, which built his house upon the sand . . .*

With the next wave, the sandy walls fell. Just like Steve's family, she thought. One day, Steve and his sisters were together; the next day, his parents divorced. Now his family was split on two continents.

She brushed the sand off her clothes and slowly walked back to the cove. What was this? A faint pattern above the water line. It looked as if someone had buried something.

Wondering what she would find, Jill used a clamshell to scrape away the sand. Eggs! A whole nest of eggs the size of Ping-Pong balls.

She called to get her parents' attention.

"You've found a turtle's nest!" her mother exclaimed, picking up an egg and examining it. Carefully she brushed away more of the sand. "Why, there must be over a hundred eggs here! Probably a green sea turtle. From the number of eggs, Mama Turtle must be a grand old lady."

Jill watched as her mother examined the nest, estimated the number of eggs, then gently covered it again. I don't understand Mom's enthusiasm, she thought. What's so great about turtles? If it were whales or manatees, I could understand. But turtles? Oh, well, I'm glad she's happy about the find.

"When will the eggs hatch, Mom?"

"It's impossible to tell exactly, but it could be any time. The incubation period is about forty-five to sixty days." She bit her lower lip in thought. "Rick, this is a good site for further study. It's too late today to do much more, so I'd like to spend another day here."

"Sounds good to me," he replied, rubbing his hand over the stubble on his chin. "I'd like to check fluid levels. This will give me a chance."

"And I'd like to do some diving," Jill said.

Above the beach, under the lengthening shadows of palms, she built a fire of driftwood and coconut husks. When the embers were hot, her father grilled generous portions of the albacore she had caught that morning.

"Well, I'd like to get an early start tomorrow," her mother said, as they finished eating.

The coals sizzled and smoked as Jill doused the flames with water. She poked the soggy ashes with a stick to make sure the fire was out. "I think I'll camp here tonight."

"Aha! A night alone without the kid!" her father said. "Maybe you should pitch a tent. I haven't seen any mosquitoes or sand fleas, but a cold centipede or scorpion might want to share your warm sleeping bag."

"Don't forget, Jill. You promised to catch up on your history," her mother said.

She groaned. "I'll get my book."

Just before nightfall, she set up the tent, and her parents took the dinghy back to the sailboat. The anchor light flickered on, twinkling as the boat rocked gently on the calm waters of the cove.

She walked along the beach, stepping over a small crab that scuttled between her feet. A quarter moon and bright stars appeared, reflecting on the bay.

Reluctantly, she remembered her promise to study. She climbed the slope to her campsite and flopped down on her sleeping bag. Guess I'd better study before I get too sleepy, she thought.

She set up a small floodlight, then began reading where she'd stopped earlier. She read about Adolf Hitler's dreaded battleship, the ironclad *Bismarck*, and how British warships bombarded and sank it.

When the words began to blur together, she rolled over and closed her eyes. A moment later, she sat up and reached for her bag. She felt around until she found what she was looking for. The manicure kit still smelled like cheese, but its colors were enchanting: South Seas Coral, Peachy Peach, Really Red, Rosewater Pink, and Purple Passion. There was even a bottle of clear polish with silver stars.

Slowly she painted her nails Really Red, despairing when the small brush slipped out of the margins. Painting the fingernails of her left hand was hard enough, but painting her right hand was impossible.

She finally gave up and blew on the wet nails. The clear coat with silver stars slipped on with less trouble. She held up her left hand and inspected it critically. Nice!

She fell asleep wondering what Steve would think about her new look, but then she slept restlessly, dreaming that scorpions were swarming over the tent. They pushed against the netting, crawled up the sides, and dropped with sinister *plop-plop* sounds onto the ground.

In her dream she saw the largest scorpion feel along the edges of the tent with its pincers until it found a small hole. It crawled into the tent and whipped its barbed tail forward, ready to strike.

Hundreds of scorpions followed. They whispered, "Let us in. Please. It's cold outside."

Realizing she was dreaming, she struggled to awake. Finally she opened her eyes.

Then she heard it again. That crawling, scratching, and rustling. As her eyes adjusted to the light, she saw the netting move. Behind it were dark, scrambling bodies. They were round, no more than two inches long, with small heads, little black flippers, and dark green shells.

Baby turtles!

She shook her head and rubbed her eyes, but this time she wasn't dreaming. By now, dozens of the tiny creatures toppled over each other, pawing at the tent.

Oh, no! she thought. They're not trying to get in. They're trying to reach my light.

Quickly she switched it off. She waited in the darkness until the turtles left, then she unzipped the tent and stepped out. On the beach below, the hatchlings headed toward the moon's reflection on the ocean.

As she watched them scoot into the water, a faint scratching noise caught her attention. She flicked on her penlight. One turtle, not much more than an inch long, had fallen into a crab hole. It looked up at her, eyes fixed on the light.

"Lucky turtle!" She picked up the infant and cupped it in her hand. "If that crab had been home, you would be history." She held it for a moment, then put it on the slope facing the beach.

"Go on. Catch up with them. I'd let you hitchhike, but I might step on one of your poky brothers."

She made sure it was going the right way, then she stretched out on her bedroll and gazed at the moon.

Turtles weren't as fascinating as whales or manatees, but she sure wouldn't want them to become extinct.

She carefully zipped up the tent, then fell into a deep, dreamless sleep.

The next morning, Jill jogged along the beach and watched the sun rise. By the time she returned to the campsite, her father had built a fire, and her mother was examining the empty nest.

Jill began to strike the tent when she remembered the bright red nails on her left hand. If she could get the polish off before—

"Hey, is that some kind of new international distress signal?"

She winced and crossed her arms to hide the offending hand. "No, I cut myself while I was reading."

"Well," her father said, raising his voice, "it looks nice. Why don't you see if you can make both hands match?"

I'll bet Dad wonders why I polished my nails in the middle of nowhere, she thought, blushing. She poured polish remover over the nails, using almost the entire bottle. Then she took down the tent.

"Hungry?" Her father asked. At least he didn't mention the polish again or look at her hand.

She eyed the ham and eggs frying in the big iron skillet.

He grinned. "I shot a canned ham and dug up some turtle eggs this morning."

She shook her head and suppressed a laugh, not daring to look at her mother.

Her mother arched an eyebrow, placed a hand on one hip, and stared at him without blinking. "Do you see a smile on this face, Rick? You would be in the frying pan—not cooking with it—if I didn't know those were chicken eggs."

He flipped an egg and chuckled. "You marine biologists are a mean group at sunrise." He sighed. "Quick, Jill! Get the skipper some coffee before she makes one of us walk the gangplank."

"Hmm." Her mother knelt to study the tracks in the sand. "I can't figure this out. The eggs hatched last night, and the tracks go in circles. The hatchlings should have headed straight for the water."

"Well, I do know a thing or two." Jill smiled sheepishly.

"For your detective mom," her father said, "a mere clue or two will do."

"I bounced a light off the sides of the tent so I could read." Jill said. "History. Like I said I would."

"Oh, so the hatchlings didn't know which way to go. They would normally head for the reflection of the moonlight on the water."

Jill nodded. "When I saw what was happening, I turned off the light."

"That explains it. This seems to be a good nesting site. We found two more nests this morning. What did the hatchlings look like?"

"Well, they were small, green, mean, and they attacked in the middle of the night."

Her mother shook her head and laughed.

As they ate, Jill made amends for teasing by describing the turtles as carefully as she could. After she'd devoured the last slice of pan-toasted bread, she asked, "Dad, how about snorkel cruising?"

"Sure."

They walked to the dinghy, and Jill pulled her gear from a faded sea bag: a facemask, a J-shaped tube with a soft-rubber mouthpiece, and black, full-foot rubber fins.

As she slipped on a buoyancy compensator, or B.C., and buckled on her weight belt, she remembered the warnings about tropical waters and coral reefs. Warnings about sharks too old and too slow to chase fish. Stonefish with deadly venomous spines. Fire coral that inflicted painful burns.

"This is paradise," her father said, as if reading her thoughts, "but it has its share of serpents. Always dive with a partner. And keep your hands out of dark holes."

Jill attached the snorkel tube to her facemask, pulled on the mask, and slipped in the mouthpiece. She pushed her feet into the rubber fins, then pulled up the heels. Finally, she strapped a stainless steel knife with a five-inch blade inside the calf of her right leg, more as a tool for prying than for protection.

Once she was waist deep in water, she propelled herself over the surface with strong, steady kicks.

The bright sunlight filtered beneath the clear waters of the cove, revealing an explosion of color that surpassed anything she had ever seen. She floated above the coral and algae, gently moving her fins.

Beneath her, fish of every possible pattern darted and wriggled in an underwater garden of brightly colored coral, lacy fans, and waving anemone. Fat black fish with round red spots. Slender, flashy gold fish. Splotchy red fish. Black-banded fish. Thin, peppermint-striped fish.

They spent the rest of the morning exploring, then they gathered shrimp for their noon meal. Her father pointed out sea cucumbers and suggested she might want some to go with the shrimp.

"Sea cucumbers?" she asked. "I don't eat vegetables that swim."

"No problem. They're really worms, not veggies. Many people consider them delicacies. Now, if you cook them with a little basil—"

She swam in the opposite direction before he could finish.

That afternoon, they stir-fried the shrimp with string beans. Even canned green beans, Jill thought, have to be better than sea worms, no matter how fresh they are.

Since her mother had the data that she needed, they prepared to leave after lunch. They rinsed and stored the equipment, placed it in a watertight chest, then turned the dinghy toward the *Sailfish*.

This, Jill thought, as she watched the island fade behind the stern, is what I would like to do for the rest of my life.

She briefly wondered where the small turtle she had helped was, then sighed, propped her elbow on the back of the seat that circled the cockpit well, and opened her history book.

Danger in Paradise

CHAPTER 07

The *Sailfish* stopped several more times to refuel, but not at ports mentioned to Björnson.

On a map, Jill's mother had drawn red circles around a dozen islands. After many days at sea, they were near those red-marked areas.

Four of the islands were unsuitable for turtle nests. One had a large colony of sea birds that would eat the hatchlings. The others were surrounded by coral reefs too high to let turtles swim ashore and lay their eggs.

The night before their next stop, Jill set her alarm so she could get up early. What will this island look like, she wondered. Can't wait to explore!

Before her parents awoke the next morning, she bounded up the companionway to watch the sun rise. To her right, the island's central peak ended in a steep cliff that dropped straight into the ocean. Circling the island was a reef that supported a half-dozen small islands like charms on a bracelet.

She smelled the aroma of bacon before her parents joined her. Dad carried a breakfast tray.

"How about a bacon, lettuce, tomato sandwich with no lettuce and tomato?" asked her mother.

"Thanks, Mom!" She gratefully accepted a sandwich and a mug of orange juice. As they enjoyed the cool morning breeze, her father led the family in devotions.

Afterwards, they swung the *Sailfish* around the island to check the charts against depth readings. The windward shore was as harsh and arid as the sheltered side was luxuriant. They circled back while Jill took depth readings. She found only two passageways through the reef that were deep enough for the dinghy. They noted the deepest channel, then dropped anchor.

The small boat was pulled alongside and loaded with test equipment, snorkeling gear, and an ice chest. As they approached the line of breakers, their boat bobbing on the growing swells, her father throttled the engine to ride with a large wave. Like surfers, they shot through the channel, their clothes damp with spray and a deafening roar in their ears.

"That was fun!" Jill shouted. "Let's do it again."

"Is that the way a member of a research team is supposed to talk?" her father teased.

Her mother laughed. "Rick, that *was* fun! May we do it again?"

He grinned, shaking his head in disbelief, then turned out of the churning waters toward the shoreline.

By early afternoon, they had collected the data. Her mother sat in the shade and wrote entries in her log, but Jill and her father pulled on their masks and fins. As they stood by the lagoon, he pointed toward the spot where they'd shot through the reef. "See the channel we came through? The surf is darker and flatter. Remember what I told you about rip currents?"

"A rip current is caused when water going back to the sea is forced through narrow channels," Jill recited. "Like running too much water through a small hose too fast. The force is increased."

"Good comparison. We'll snorkel in this area. Stay away from the far end of the lagoon where channels cut through the reef."

Jill nodded. "My diving teacher always said, 'Enjoy the ocean, but don't ever get careless.' "

Although the weather was warm and the sun hot, they wore wet suits to protect their skin from the sharp coral. For a close look at the seabed, Jill deflated her buoyancy compensator and pushed herself beneath the surface. She descended at a sharp angle.

It's like falling headfirst into a kaleidoscope, she thought.

She floated over pale green coral shaped like massive elk antlers and orange-red coral that resembled clusters of mushrooms. A cream-colored coral looked like a human brain. When her father wrote BRAIN CORAL on his underwater slate, she laughed, exhaling a cloud of bubbles.

Needing air, she pushed toward the surface. A few feet above her, a cloud of dainty, silver-blue fish scattered like windblown raindrops.

She broke the surface, exhaling with a sharp blast that forced water out of the snorkel. Breathing deeply several times, she dove again, this time almost smacking a speckled brown fish grazing over algae-coated coral.

"Look!" Jill signaled to her father. She pressed two fingers to her right eye and pointed with her left index finger to a tiny fish with orange and white bands. The small fish wriggled like bait, luring a much larger fish into an anemone's swaying tentacles. Then the small fish disappeared, leaving the victim to be paralyzed by the anemone.

For the next hour, they cruised the lagoon surface and explored its depths. She was eyeing an odd coral formation when she saw her father urgently signal "Danger. Return to point of entry."

Must be too near the rip current, she thought, as she kicked toward the surface. She pictured in her mind the low reef on the north end of the lagoon. Water that washed over the reef returned hard and fast through the narrow trenches.

Just then, she saw a Portuguese man-of-war between herself and the water's surface. Its trailing tentacles moved slowly as if searching for prey. The creature looked as harmless as a big soap bubble, but it was armed with poisonous stinging cells.

Even my knife won't help, she thought. Can't touch the tentacles! Hold breath. Duck clear. Now! Kick toward the surface. Finally, air!

She exhaled sharply to clear the snorkel, took a deep breath, then gasped as her right hand and wrist exploded with pain. The man-of-war! She recoiled and cradled her right hand. It felt as though she had touched a red-hot burner. Then she saw her father urgently signal "Stop!"

It was too late. She had pushed back into the rip current.

A strong surge of water spun her around. It slammed her against the reef. Churning waves closed over her head. The current dragged her backwards and upside down through the murky water. She couldn't see. She couldn't breathe.

She released the clasp on her weight belt as she tumbled along the ocean floor, scraped against gritty sand and sharp coral. Her lungs burned, and she swallowed salt water.

As she felt herself losing consciousness, something thrust her through the reef, into the open sea. She gasped for air and coughed. Her mask and fins were gone, but her head was above water because of the buoyancy compensator.

She gulped air, grateful just to breathe. Too tired to swim, she let the current pull her. Her eyes, nose, and lungs burned, and she coughed violently.

As she became more aware of what had happened, she tried to think. *Lord, you know where I am. Please help me!*

A rip current? My head hurts. Rip current . . . swept out to sea. Something I'm supposed to remember . . . Don't fight it. That's it. Don't fight the current. When the current weakens, I can swim toward shore.

Through blurred eyes, she watched the island shrinking. I wonder if Dad is all right, she thought.

A calmness settled over her, and she remembered her training. She rode outgoing waves until the current weakened. Then, still coughing up salt water, she swam shoreward, blocking out the pain, her eyes fixed on the nearest outlying island.

She didn't realize how tired she was until she saw the white hull of their dinghy as it cut through the swells. Painfully, she raised her right arm to wave.

Strong arms pulled her from the water. She shook with cold despite the large beach towel that her father wrapped around her. "Thank you, Lord," he murmured.

"Gear . . . mask . . . fins . . . gone," she said, coughing. She winced as her mother smoothed her hair back to check a gash on her forehead.

"Equipment's replaceable. You're not."

"You couldn't have handled it any better," her father said, his low-pitched voice huskier than usual. "You kept your head. You dropped your weight belt. You didn't fight the current."

Jill grimaced. "Don't like losing."

"I don't either, Jill," her father said. His gray eyes clouded with concern, and he turned the boat back toward the *Sailfish*.

Within minutes they were onboard. Her mother pulled on lab gloves and picked the bluish-green pieces of tentacle from her hand and arm. She rinsed the welts with salt water.

"If any stinging cells are still sticking to your skin, fresh water will cause the cells to release acid," she explained.

She treated a heavily bleeding cut on Jill's left shoulder and checked for broken bones. "No broken bones, Jill, but your arms and chest are one big black bruise. Reminds me of your first bicycle ride. Now, how did you cut your forehead and shoulder?"

"I—I got scraped on the reef." All too vividly Jill recalled the dark, gritty water pulling her under.

"Can you stand for me to clean this up?"

"I have a choice?"

"No."

Jill drank a cup of steaming hot tomato soup, then her mother gave her an antihistamine tablet and applied salve to her blistered hand.

"Okay," she said finally. "I'll leave you alone in just a minute." She shone a penlight into each of Jill's eyes.

"Doctors make boat calls?" Jill asked, beginning to feel more like herself. Then she looked down at the cabin floor. "Mom, I almost gave up. God helped me, didn't He?"

"Yes, He did," her mother said. "We've prayed for His protection on this trip . . ."

She didn't finish. Instead, her eyes wet with tears, she kissed Jill on the cheek.

The
Storm

CHAPTER 08

Jill yawned and glanced at the digital watch on her wrist. It was 5:30 A.M., lunch time back home, allowing for the time zone difference. Right about now, she thought, Chip is banging her dish around, hinting for something to eat.

As she took a quick shower, she wondered how her marine fish were, especially the sea horses, those fussy eaters. Getting ready, she tried to run a brush through her curly hair, then clambered barefoot onto the deck.

The morning air felt damp. The sky was hazy, and a faint halo circled the dimly glowing sun. The *Sailfish* was under full sail, and the spinnaker bulged with the morning breeze.

Her father sat at the helm. He was humming snatches of a hymn. " 'In ev'ry high and stormy gale, my anchor holds . . . on Christ, the solid Rock, I stand.' " He greeted her with a smile.

"Avast ye swab," said her mother. She was in the cockpit, her Bible in one hand and ice water in the other. Weeks at sea had lightened her dark hair, adding reddish-gold highlights. A sun visor, dark glasses, and a tan had become a permanent part of her features.

"Are we on schedule?" Jill asked.

"Aye, aye. Just checked our position. We'll make landfall by noon, Matey, if'n the winds blow fair and pirates don't thwart us."

"All right, Mom. All right. Hey, what are you and Dad going to do when we get back to the real world?"

She shook her head resignedly. "Same as you, I guess. Or maybe we'll take up residence in the South Pacific, join pirates, and roam the wide seas in search of gold doubloons and jewels worth a king's ransom."

Jill raised an eyebrow, shook her head, and turned toward the cabin. "Pirates don't hire people who run around the world saving turtles," she said with a smile.

"If they're pirates who like turtles, they do!"

Jill grabbed a bag of potato chips, sprawled on her berth, and opened a book. Next island-stop is today, she thought. And I will *not* be stuck on this boat finishing lessons—like the last two times.

She was especially restless because she'd been confined while recovering from her run-in with the rip current and the Portuguese man-of-war. As for the man-of-war, well, she'd seen several of them since then, and she'd decided that if her parents ever wanted to save those UFO's (Ugly Floating Objects), she would draw the line. Too bad they aren't extinct, she thought.

She looked at the abrasions on her arms and legs. Better, much better. The swelling is gone, the black bruises are greenish-yellow, and the cuts are healing. Maybe I can dive again soon.

Now she wished that she'd finished her scuba certification so she'd have more diving freedom than snorkeling offered. Setting aside thoughts of islands, jellyfish, and diving, she sighed and turned to the next chapter with one goal: Finish quickly.

Before she realized it, three hours had passed. Her stomach felt as empty as the crumpled chip bag. She wondered why no one had fixed lunch, then checked the job list.

Oops! My turn, she realized. No wonder I'm starving. Bet Mom and Dad are too.

She hurriedly dumped canned tuna into a bowl, added green globs of pickle relish, mashed them together with mayonnaise, and smeared the sticky mixture on bread.

With a bag of cookies between her teeth, canned sodas under her arms, and sandwiches in her hands, she moved cautiously to the deck. As she stepped into the cockpit well, the boat rocked to one side, and she fell, clutching for the railing.

The tuna sandwiches flew over the side.

"Fish food," she grumbled. "And all that time cooking from scratch."

Her mother sat nearby at the wheel, but she didn't seem to notice Jill's fall.

Jill captured the sodas that were rolling around the cockpit. "Here's lunch—what's left of it," she said, holding up the bag of cookies and a drink.

Her mother was studying the instruments, and she didn't seem to be listening. Jill leaned over her shoulder, looking at the gauges.

"Wind direction has shifted, and the barometer is falling—falling rapidly," her mother murmured. "We may be in for some rough weather." They watched her father as he walked unsteadily from the bow of the ship to the cockpit.

"There's a change in wind strength and direction," he said, taking off his sunglasses and rubbing his eyes. "What are the barometer and anemometer readings?"

"The barometric pressure shows a high rate of fall." Jill's mother ran her index finger over the recorded readings. "The wind's stiffened from ten to fourteen knots in the last three minutes."

She looked at her husband, then down at the instrument panel again. "And still rising. Make that ten to sixteen knots in the last three minutes."

"How far are we from the nearest island?" he asked.

She pushed back her wind-tangled hair and stared at the thin pencil line that marked their progress on the chart.

"I think I made a sighting a few minutes ago," she said, handing him the binoculars. "See what you think."

He focused the binoculars and searched the horizon. He stood motionless for a moment, then nodded his agreement. He looked back at Jill. "Initiate the bad weather procedure."

"Okay, Dad."

He gave her a tight smile. "Break out foul weather gear. We each need a slicker, a life belt, and a lifeline. Then go below deck. Fill one Thermos with soup and another with coffee. Make sure nothing's lying around. After you've stowed everything—books, cups, pencils, anything loose—join me on deck."

Jill nodded. It felt good to be part of the action, but what would the next hour bring?

DANGER FOLLOWS

The sea had roughened by the time she finished below. The overcast sky was growing darker. On deck she clipped her belt to the lifeline and, pushed by the rising winds, inched down the length of the hull to the bow. Her father had furled the spinnaker and taken two reefs in the mainsail.

"I'll finish here," he shouted over the rising wind. "We may switch to auxiliary. Make sure we're not trailing any lines that could get tangled in the propeller, then help your mother. She has her hands full just managing the helm."

Jill had trouble keeping her balance because of the rise and fall of the deck. Dark, threatening waves rocked the boat. As thunderclouds boiled overhead and the temperature dropped, she shivered, grateful for her rain gear.

After checking to make sure no lines dragged overboard, Jill clipped her life harness to a deck fitting and sat beside her mother. She said nothing to distract her. At their present speed, taking a steep wave in the wrong way would send tons of water crashing down on them.

Her mother handed her a chart. "See that island?" She pointed to a small, irregular circle on the map. "We need to drop anchor on the side away from the wind. And we need to stay off the rocks."

Jill studied the chart, checking the currents and the water depth. She squinted through binoculars at a hazy gray blur until it became more distinct.

"Are we going to anchor near the island?"

"That depends on the strength of the wind and the shoreline. I would like to anchor the boat and take refuge on the island. But unless the wind drops, we won't dare get that close."

"Here's a cove, Mom. No strong currents or underwater obstructions." She pointed to a spot on the chart.

"That will do. Help watch the instruments. Especially the depth."

"I'll be careful. It's not a good day for swimming."

Her mother smiled, then turned her full attention to the helm.

As the blasting wind kicked up steeper waves, Jill's father motioned for her help. They furled the mainsail that flapped as if it would tear into shreds. The *Sailfish* rode bare-masted on auxiliary power through the angry waves. With an eerie wail, the wind whistled through the naked poles and shrouds.

When the island emerged from the dark horizon, Jill was awed by the severity of the jagged peaks. Large breakers beat against the cliffs.

The waves grew larger, washing over the deck. We're racing against time, Jill thought. If we don't get the *Sailfish* moored, we'll smack those cliffs. And I'll be standing on a stack of lumber instead of a deck.

She trailed a sea anchor, a canvas bag, from the bow to keep the head of the *Sailfish* turned into the wind. As the boat neared shallower water, she dropped a ground anchor, allowing plenty of line to run out.

The wind moaned through the bare rigging. The sky darkened, the ocean foamed, and lightning pierced the sky. Then the storm broke in full fury over them, and they were caught in a heavy downpour.

Jill clutched the railing to keep from falling overboard. She glanced at her father. The color was drained beneath his tan. His mouth was drawn in a tight line.

He mouthed the words, "Let's go below," but she could not hear his voice. As the deck pitched beneath her feet, she eased to the forward hatch, clutching the railing, and dropped into the forward cabin. Her father closed the hatch tightly behind them.

Shaky from her battle with the wind, Jill shed her wet slicker and sipped the hot soup she had heated earlier. The waves sprayed the portholes with foam.

As the bow of the boat plunged and rose, the cabin floor pitched beneath her feet. The soup mug flew from her hands and bounced off the wall. She braced herself to keep from being thrown across the room.

A wise man . . . built his house upon a rock . . . rain descended . . . floods came, and the winds blew, and beat upon that house; and it fell not: for it was founded upon a rock. The Rock. Christ, the Son of God.

"Doesn't feel like I'm on the Rock, right now," she whispered, "but I thank You, God, because I am."

DANGER FOLLOWS

By morning, the storm had passed. Jill and her mother went ashore while her father stayed behind to work on the engine.

What a gloomy island, she thought, as she looked up at the jagged, mist-covered peaks.

While her mother took samples, she explored the narrow black beach. It was littered with debris from the storm. Rainwater puddled in crevices and gushed through cracks in the volcanic rock. Amid the seaweed were sea creatures, living and dead: shells, snails, starfish, and dried sponges.

At Jill's feet, trapped in a tidal pool, was a small silver fish. She dug a trench in the sand with her fingers, and the fish darted back toward the lagoon.

Jill eyed the crystal water longingly. It's not a very big lagoon, she thought. Maybe as wide as an Olympic-sized pool. Clear. A great place to dive. Hope Mom will think I'm well enough.

In a tangle of seaweed, she found a brown-and-pink shell called a chiragra spider. The shell was empty, so she brushed off the sand. It would look great in her aquarium.

What was this? She kneeled to look at pieces of charred driftwood scattered near a stone-lined pit. Someone had cooked a meal here. Who was it? How long ago? She picked up a piece of the burnt wood. It wasn't driftwood. Puzzled, she strode back to the dinghy.

Her mother was sitting on a large rock, writing in her logbook. When she saw Jill, she laid the book aside and walked down the beach to meet her.

"What's on the lunch menu, Mom?"

"Peanut butter and jelly—or jelly and peanut butter."

"I think I'd rather have the jelly and peanut butter. How about candy corn for dessert?"

"Yes, please," her mother replied. "What's that you're holding?"

"I found this near a hole in the ground. It was lined with stones. Like a cooking pit."

"Hmm. Looks like a broken oar."

"Who do you think made the pit?"

Her mother shook her head. "I don't know. This isn't the kind of place you would come to on purpose. Dark. Bleak. Sparse vegetation."

Jill looked at the oar. "I wonder if the person who used this is still here. If you had no way of leaving this island—"

A large drop of water splattered on her forehead. She wiped it off and eyed the gathering clouds. "Not more rain! Is it going to storm again?"

"Your guess is as good as mine. Let's take our lunch and go." Her mother looked back at the rock where she'd been sitting. She paused, looking puzzled. "Did you see my log?"

"Did you pack it up?"

"I don't know. I suppose I did." She frowned. "Come on. Let's get back to the boat before it rains."

Tevake

CHAPTER 09

After Jill and her mother left the beach, an old man, who'd been sitting in the shadow of the rock, stood to his feet.

Tall and muscular, with brown skin and straight, short-cropped gray hair, he wore only a breechcloth. Geometric tattoos covered the weathered skin on his arms and shoulders.

Tevake slipped the book he was holding into a shoulder pouch. He waited until Jill and her mother had boarded the *Sailfish*, then he turned back toward the cliff and climbed straight up. At twenty feet above the beach, he pulled himself onto an overhanging ledge and crawled through a narrow breach in the rocks. After traveling over a narrow trail through the jagged peaks, he stood on a precipice overlooking a green valley.

Beside him, a waterfall dropped a thousand feet into a deep pool, and beyond the pool grazed a small herd of horses. He watched the horses for a moment, then skirted the waterfall and descended the steep slope. A stallion looked up as the man approached a copper-colored mare nursing a colt. Tevake spoke softly to the mare, then dropped an armful of grass near her forefeet.

As if a hole had been punched in the heavens, the rain began to fall, at first lightly, then harder and faster. Tevake broke off a large leaf and held it over his head. As he followed a worn trail through the thick foliage, a small pig emerged from the undergrowth and followed him. On the other side of the valley, he pushed aside a tangle of vines to reveal an opening between two rock columns.

Once inside the cave, he built a fire to roast his meal of fish. As he ate, he shared scraps with the pig which grunted contentedly.

DANGER FOLLOWS

Working by firelight, Tevake used a handmade adz to shape a steering paddle. He inspected it, then laid it beside stout poles he had cut to replace the mast and spars of an outrigger canoe.

He threw a few husks on the fire, then pulled the book out of his pouch. As he turned the pages, he scowled and muttered to himself.

After looking through the book, he returned it to the pouch. He covered himself with a mat and lay down, murmuring, "*Je bénirai l'Eternel en tout temps . . . I will bless the Lord at all times; his praise shall continually be in my mouth.*"

The heavy rain continued to fall. In the valley, the horses huddled under a rocky outcrop, seeking shelter from the downpour.

During the night, part of the mountain shuddered, shifted, then broke away. Nothing in the path of the mudslide withstood its force. The muddy torrent swept away boulders, bushes, and trees, and within seconds, it was over. A mudslide thirty feet deep sealed the opening of a tunnel through the mountain.

One minute the small colt was pressed close to his mother. The next, he had been lifted on a large wave of mud and pushed into the mouth of the tunnel.

All alone, his hindquarters buried in mud, the colt trembled. He tried to lash out with his hind legs but could not move. Frantically, he threw his weight onto his front legs and lurched forward a few inches at a time until he struggled free. His nostrils quivered as he searched for his mother's scent.

Before him was the dark tunnel and the far-off sound of rain and surf. Behind him was a wall of dirt, grass, and rock. Unable to find a way back, he turned toward the fresh air rolling in from the ocean. He walked through the tunnel, stiff-legged, cold, and trembling. Wary of the strange objects, he snuffed each one: large metal drums, discarded crates and boxes, food scraps, and oily rags.

He reached the opening of the cave, but a blast of cold wind pushed him to his knees. The rising tide surged around his hooves, and he fell again.

The rain blew in sheets. Lightning flashed and thunder split the air. He retreated, bumping into a large basket that shifted back and forth with the incoming tide. The colt poked his head inside. Here were familiar smells, the smells of fruit and dried grass. Like a small den, the basket offered refuge from the wet, cold wind. He lowered his head and squeezed into it. Dazed, he curled up for warmth and lay very still.

During the night a gust of wind caught the basket. The top blew shut, and the basket, pulled by the tide, rolled out of the mouth of the tunnel toward the beach. The colt tumbled downward, head over heels.

The roar of the ocean grew nearer. Seconds later, towering waves caught the basket, tossing it, and the warm pouch became cold. The colt shivered as his nest became damp. In spite of the violent rocking and wet chill, his eyes grew heavy. When the waves finally subsided, he fell asleep once more.

In the morning, he awoke with a start, struggling against the tight enclosure. He twisted and turned, pushing his muzzle against the cover. Finally, the top of the basket slipped off.

Blinded by the sun, he scrambled through the opening just as a wave broke over him. He tried to stand, chest deep in the water, but tottered and fell as his weak legs buckled. The next wave pushed him into a swirling backwash, pulling him under.

Working his small legs furiously, he surfaced to gulp air. Then another wave broke over him. The tide washed him onto the beach, but he lay motionless on the sand.

When Tevake awoke, the rain had stopped and the sun was shining. He threw off the mat, sat up, and fumbled in his pouch for a small book. It had the words *Nouveau Testament et Psaumes* printed on the outside. For several minutes, he stared at a photograph glued inside the cover. Then he opened the book and began to read.

After eating, he stuffed his pouch with provisions and stepped out onto a rock ledge in front of the cave. To his right, smoke drifted up the steep hillside.

The pig pushed its snout against his leg, grunting. He spoke sharply, and the small animal sat down on its hindquarters. He spoke more firmly. The pig hesitated, then scrambled back into the cave.

DANGER FOLLOWS

Tevake climbed toward the blowing wisps of smoke, holding onto rocks, roots, and vines, until he reached a peak overlooking the valley.

Lightning had struck, burning a black, smoking brand into the side of the mountain. He looked across the valley. To the right of the waterfall, everything looked as it had yesterday. To the left, part of the mountain was gone.

He scrambled down the steep incline and ran toward the mud-slide.

The horses, which usually watered and grazed near the pool in the morning, were nowhere to be seen. A section of the mountain had fallen in a mound of earth, rock, and broken limbs. The water was muddied and filled with debris. As he stooped to clear rocks and branches from the pool, he saw a flash of copper at the foot of the mudslide.

It was the mare. She lay lifeless, partially buried in the mud, her neck broken.

Not far away, leaves rustled and a twig snapped. A large clay jar appeared and seemed to float through the weeds. Muffled grunts came from inside the container. Then the weeds parted to reveal the bristly black hair of the pig with a jar wobbling on his neck. Before Tevake could grab him, the pig tumbled into the pool, splashing and stirring up silt.

The old man's sad face lightened, and he pulled the pig out. While Tevake pulled the jar off his head, the pig squealed as if he were being roasted. Finally free, the pig trotted in circles, then rolled in the grass by the pool's edge.

Tevake filled hollow gourds from the waterfall and tied them to his waist. He left the pig at the foot of the mountain and followed a twisted trail up through the jagged peaks. He returned to the ledge overlooking the cove. The boat was still there.

Red Velvet

CHAPTER 10

Jill sat up in her berth. Something had awakened her. What was it?

She heard it again. Her mother's voice, then locker doors slamming and boxes scraping across the cabin floor.

She dressed and dashed out of her cabin. Her mother was in the laboratory crawling around on her hands and knees.

"Mom! What's wrong?"

"Jill—" She pushed a strand of hair out of her face and sat down in the middle of the floor. "I can't find the logbook. Do you have any idea where I might have put it?"

"The last time I saw you with it, you were sitting on that big rock. Right before it started to rain."

Her mother sighed. "Well, I must not have packed it. It's not with the samples. Or in my briefcase. I don't know where it could be unless I dropped it on the beach."

"It rained all last night. Will your notes be okay?"

"I don't know. The cover is waterproof, but the pages certainly aren't."

Her father came down the companionway. "It's not in the dinghy."

"I have to find that log. It represents all of the work we've done. If I lose it, we might as well have been on vacation—at the university's expense."

"Do you have it on disk?" Jill asked.

"Only about one-third. I don't know what I'll do if I can't find it."

DANGER FOLLOWS

Jill's father nodded his understanding. "Let's go back. We'll help you look."

"But you still haven't found the problem with the engine. You need to be here."

"I'll work on it later." He helped her to her feet. "We need to find your log."

Jill grabbed her daypack and scrambled into the dinghy. Her father motored back to the area where her mother had worked the day before.

She had just started to help her parents search the beach when she noticed odd tracks in the wet sand. Among the prints made by sea birds, crabs, and snails were the unmistakable prints of a horse—a very small horse.

You need to be looking for the notebook, she reminded herself. But the tracks were a mystery she had to solve.

She knew that horses ran wild on some islands in the South Pacific, but this island was no paradise. It had all the charm of a rock fort. Puzzled, she followed the tracks until the ground became rocky and the tiny hoof prints disappeared.

She began to explore the rocky shoreline when she saw a glimmer of gold. How odd—a cluster of yellow feathers stuck in a bush. She reached out to pluck the feathers when she realized they were soft, like hair, and firmly attached.

When Jill pulled the colt's forelock, a copper-colored foal with a gold mane popped up, its eyes wide.

She dropped the handful of hair and stumbled backward.

The colt jumped, snorted, and trembled from the tip of his copper nose to the end of his golden tail.

For a full minute, Jill stared. She rubbed her eyes. It was still there. Wherever the animal had come from, it was a baby, alone and frightened.

She gingerly stretched out a hand, palm upward. The colt quivered but did not bolt. Jill inched closer, her hand near enough to the colt's velvet muzzle to feel his warm, moist breath.

He held one foot off the ground, and several black quills protruded from the fetlock. Dried blood caked his nose, and there were fresh cuts on his chest and legs.

So, he's caught a sea urchin, she thought. The quills are painful, but not deadly. Maybe that's when he fell and cut himself.

She pulled off her daypack, wondering if island horses liked sugar as much as continent horses. She sprinkled a few kernels of candy corn on the flat palm of her hand.

The colt looked at it curiously, sniffed, then ate the candy.

Slowly, so she wouldn't frighten him, she spilled the contents of her daypack on the ground. She selected matches, pliers, a coffee can, and a small bag of candy corn.

She dropped pieces of candy for the colt to eat as she gathered dry seaweed and driftwood to make a fire. If she soaked the colt's hoof in hot water for fifteen minutes, the pain would go away, but would he accept help?

She filled the coffee can with water from her canteen, then struck a match. The colt ignored her, nibbling the candy. She poked her finger into the water, like a parent checking a baby bottle.

She held his left hoof and pulled out the first quill. The colt trembled, but didn't flinch. Out came the second, then third quill. She tested the water again. Just right. After taking the can from the fire, she submerged the injured hoof up to the fetlock and checked her watch.

For the next quarter hour, as she held his hoof in the water, she wondered if this whole experience could possibly be a dream.

No, the colt was real, and she would probably be on the hit list of a raging red-eyed stallion, smoke pouring from its nostrils.

Wondering what to do next, Jill touched the bristly mane and stroked the little nose, careful not to touch the cut. His nose felt like soft velvet. Red velvet.

The colt broke Jill's reverie, nuzzling her hand for more treats. She dug deep into her pockets, finding shells, a handful of sand, spare double-A batteries, and a caramel, soft and sticky, from which she peeled the wrapper.

Eagerly, he nibbled the candy. The chewy stickiness seemed to bother him because he tossed his head from side to side, the sun glinting on his yellow mane.

"I think I'll call you Red. Oh, no, you don't," she said, as he pulled his injured fetlock from the water.

"Just a few more minutes." She firmly pushed the small hoof back into the water. Finally, she inspected his hoof and allowed him to take it from the water.

"Red," she mused, "what do I do with you? If there were enough food to survive here—if it looked like you belonged here—I could just go off and leave you. Where did you come from?"

The colt stood shakily on long, spindly legs. Switching his stubby tail from side to side, he shook sand off his coat much as a bird shakes off water.

"Are you an orphan? Shipwrecked? Where's your mother? Will you be okay if I leave you?"

She sighed and threw the remaining supplies into her daypack. "C'mon, Red," she called.

He was poking his nose near the ashes of the extinguished fire, and he raised his head. In his mouth was the boomerang Jill had forgotten to return to her daypack. When she bent to take it from him, the colt dropped it, snuffing her palm for candy.

"Spoiled already, huh? Come on. If I am alive, awake, and not seeing things, you have a problem. Except that, since I found you, you're kind of my problem. So, this means we both have a problem—the same problem. You."

She paused and looked over her shoulder to make sure he was following. "Of course, we need to keep you in your natural habitat, but where is it? First, let's find out if anyone else can see you."

As she rounded a weather-beaten cluster of palms, she saw her parents, down near the shore. Oh, no, she thought. I forgot. I was supposed to help look for the log.

She held her breath and fumbled self-consciously with the boomerang and the straps on her daypack as she drew closer. She waited for their reaction to the colt.

"Find anything yet?" her father asked.

"Well, I—"

Why didn't Dad say something about the colt?

"I did find something," she said, after an awkward pause.

"Well," her mother said, "I didn't know you had lost it, but the loss of your souvenir is hardly comparable to the loss of my research notes."

"Souvenir?"

"Your boomerang. You found it. Very good. Now please put it up and help us look."

"I don't mean this—I mean that," she said, gesturing behind her. But there was no colt. Nothing with four legs was anywhere to be seen.

Her father stopped searching for the logbook. Jill recognized the look he gave her. She had seen it often in the two weeks since she had been thrown against the reef, hitting her head.

"He's not here!" Jill exclaimed.

"Uh, who's not here?" her father asked. He ran his fingers through his hair.

"Th—the horse."

"There's no horse here," her mother said softly. She looked like she was going to cry. She glanced sideways at her husband. "Jill, you look flushed. Sit down. Why don't you drink something cold?" She pulled a chilled soda from the ice chest.

"Wait a minute," her father said. "Do you mean you've seen a horse on this beach?"

She bit her lip and nodded. "A reddish-colored colt. He has a yellow mane and tail. He was hiding in a bush."

Now, that really sounds dumb, she thought.

Confused, she turned and stared at the black, sandy slope edged with coarse grass. The island suddenly seemed very quiet, except for the rumble of the surf and the startled squawk of a chicken.

A chicken?

For the second time that day, she saw a fleeting glimpse of gold. Without explanation, she scrambled over scattered driftwood, up the slope to the rock where her mother had been sitting the day before.

Jill laughed, ecstatic with relief. "There you are!" she exclaimed. The small colt followed as she emerged from behind the rock, and her parents were clearly surprised.

After a long pause, her mother exclaimed, "It's beautiful! Where did it come from? This is an uninhabitable island. Narrow beach. Volcanic cliffs. Not enough plant life to support a—a goat." She reached out to touch the colt, but he squealed, then bolted.

Jill threw her arms around his neck to restrain him. Her mother stepped back, tripped over the ice chest, and fell into the water. The colt wriggled out of Jill's embrace and tumbled into her mother's lap. He regained his balance, and still limping, ran from the water toward a rocky ridge.

Jill jumped to her feet and ran after him. A small lizard dashed in front of the colt and squeezed under a piece of gnarled driftwood. The colt craned his neck to see underneath and came face-to-face with a coconut crab swinging its pincers.

Jill grabbed the colt, pulling his head away from the giant crab.

"That," she said, "you don't mess with. A crab that big will rearrange your face. You should see what he can do to a tin can!"

She twisted her fingers in the golden mane, guiding the colt back to the dinghy. She felt as happy as the day she'd picked Chip, a tiny grey ball of fur, from a litter of puppies.

Her parents had stopped looking for the logbook, and they greeted her with disbelieving shakes of the head.

"Mom, do you think he's hungry?"

"Most infants are always hungry."

"I've been thinking about that," her father said. He tore off a corner of a towel, twisted it, and dipped it into a can of evaporated milk. "This is not going to be his preferred brand." He grinned and handed Jill the milk.

If the canned, sun-warmed milk wasn't what the colt wanted, she couldn't tell by the way he pulled on the milk-soaked towel. He trembled at the smell of the milk and drank so quickly that it drizzled down the front of his chest.

"We can rig up a better bottle on the *Sailfish*," her father said as they watched him drink.

Jill tried not to react, but her hopes, against all reason, soared. He'd said, "on the *Sailfish*!" Maybe, just maybe . . .

But she knew that a sailboat was no place for a colt that chased lizards and sea urchins. She could imagine Red kicking a hole in the satellite navigation monitor or skidding off the deck. And there would be no way to feed him when they ran out of evaporated milk.

Chip would've been happy to eat nachos and carob cookies forever, but sooner or later, Red would turn into a large, grass-eating horse.

No Easy Answers

CHAPTER 11

Jill sat near the colt, stroking its downy nose. She pretended not to see the glance her parents exchanged. Her mother's forehead had a wrinkled, worried look, but her father's gray eyes danced with amusement.

"Looks like an endangered species to me," he said. "Parents and origin unknown. Red rates at least a line in your next paper on turtles: 'Tired turtle team touts tale of tiny orphaned trotter.' "

"Rick!" her mother protested.

Jill could almost read their faces. Mom doesn't want to leave the colt, she thought, but this is one specimen that won't fit in a plastic bag, a beaker, or on her laboratory shelves. And Dad! He's got to find a safe beach for a turtle hatchery—and keep us out of danger.

She knew her parents could deal with tough problems, but finding an orphaned animal—a potentially large one—on a research trip was a challenge.

Finally her father broke the strained silence. A wry, lopsided smile tilted his mouth. "No decision has to be made right now. With the problems we're having, we can't go anywhere today, anyway. I'll make a quick trip to the *Sailfish*. There's got to be a better way to feed a colt than drowning him in canned milk."

Jill looked at him in surprise. "Since we're not leaving, I'd like to camp out tonight."

"Fine. That engine has to be fixed before we can leave." He gestured toward the small lagoon. "Looks like a good place to swim—that is, if your doctor releases you."

DANGER FOLLOWS

Jill looked at her mother, who gave her thumbs up.

While her father took the dinghy back to the *Sailfish*, her mother continued to comb the area where she had been working.

Jill stayed beside the sleeping colt. She clasped her hands around her knees, listening to the surf. Their trip had proved wilder than she could have imagined.

And the future still held danger. She was sure the muscleman with shark-eyes had caused their fuel shortage. Had they gotten away from him? She stroked the soft hair on the colt's neck. What would they do with this little creature who had kicked a dent in her heart?

She leaned back, looking up at the massive cliffs. Solid rock. *Whosoever heareth these sayings of mine, and doeth them, I will liken him unto a wise man, which built his house upon a rock.*

Lord, she prayed, help me to remember the Rock. Help me trust You.

Just then, a dislodged stone tumbled down the face of the cliff. Startled, she thought she saw the shadow of a human form on the ledge above her. She squinted to see more clearly, but the shadow was gone.

"Someone throwing rocks at you?" Her father had returned in the dinghy.

"I hope not," she said with a nervous laugh. "Could the person who made the fire pit and the broken paddle still be here?"

"That's doubtful. But that colt came from somewhere, and he hasn't been here long." Her father studied the cliff with a thoughtful expression on his face. "We don't have a detailed map of this island because we didn't plan to stop here." He handed Jill a Thermos filled with warm water and powdered milk. "Give this a try." For a nipple, he'd brought a rubber glove.

"This baby bottle looks weird, but it works," she said.

"So I see. What he can't finish, put in the ice chest. We'll set up the tent for you."

By the time her parents made camp, the colt had swallowed the contents of the bottle and was still greedily pulling at the nipple.

Something had been nagging at the back of Jill's mind. She figured out what it was while she was feeding the colt. "Dad, are you going to be here for a while?"

"A little while longer, to help your mom. And I'd like to put something in my stomach besides a peanut butter and jelly sandwich."

"Before it gets dark, I want to backtrack to where I found the colt. And I'd rather not take him."

Her father nodded. "He does have a knack for getting into trouble."

Jill retraced the path she had taken earlier. She walked above the water line, looking for clues to the colt's mysterious appearance.

The beach quickly narrowed, giving way to cliff walls that rose straight out of the ocean. How, she wondered, did he end up here, between cliffs and the ocean on a skinny strip of sand? She walked back to the palm tree and the thicket where the colt had hidden. Pale flowers clung to the bush like tattered yellow ribbons.

She waded in the surf to skirt a large chunk of volcanic rock, then stopped. On one side was the ocean. On the other was a cliff. Trapped in a tidal pool at the foot of the cliff was a large handwoven basket.

Well, I'm finding everything but the kitchen sink—and mom's logbook, she thought. Her curiosity grew as she examined the bulky, watermelon-shaped basket. Unable to go farther, she turned back, taking it with her.

When she returned, her father was scaling fish, and her mother was feeding driftwood to a fire. They must have stopped searching for the log. Red was nearby, pawing holes in the wet sand. The colt turned his head at the sound of Jill's greeting.

"Well," her father said, as he examined the basket, "I haven't seen anything like this since I disarmed a World War II relic—a torpedo—in the South Pacific. I was in the Marianas investigating reports that villagers were using a torpedo for a park bench. While I was there, I had the chance to watch an age-old art—shipbuilding, Polynesian style."

He ran his fingers over the inside of the basket. "You see this? It's caulked—waterproofed—with heated breadfruit sap."

He pulled out a short length of rope that was woven into the basket. "This rope is made of sennit—hand-rolled coconut-husk fibers."

"Rick, do you think there's a connection?"

"Between the colt and this basket? Who knows? It certainly doesn't answer any questions for us."

"Dad, if there's a connection between the colt and the basket, I'll rename him Moses." Jill looked inside the basket, felt around, and pulled out several strands of gold hair.

"Mom, could you check to see if these match Red's hair?"

"We can see if it's similar—when more important matters are resolved."

While they talked, her father rolled some fish in flour, added a dash of salt and ground pepper, and sizzled the fillets in an iron skillet until they turned golden brown.

Long after they had eaten, they sat near the warmth of the fire.

"What if God doesn't answer a prayer?" Jill asked. "Or if He doesn't answer a prayer the way a person wants Him to?"

"That's where faith comes in," her mother said. "Remember the day you took your cousins to the amusement park? How Adelaide begged to ride the roller coaster, but you wouldn't take her?"

Jill smiled at the memory. "That coaster goes upside down and backwards. She was so mad at me! But if I'd taken her, she would've been scared to death." She looked at the colt sleeping beside her. "I see what you mean. I wasn't trying to hurt Addie's feelings, but she didn't understand."

Her father threw wood on the flames. The fire sparked and crackled. "God loves you and cares about every area of your life. He even knows how many hairs you have on your head. That's close attention to detail."

Her parents took the dinghy back to the *Sailfish*, leaving Jill with the colt. She propped her chin on her hands, watching the anchor lights come on. The forward light flickered on and off several times, then went out. Better check that tomorrow, she thought. One more problem.

Early the next morning she awoke. Shivering, she pulled the warm sleeping bag up over her head. Suddenly she remembered the events of the day before and sat straight up.

"Red," she whispered, looking at the small colt, "you had a rough day for such a little fellow." To avoid waking him, she eased out of the tent.

She walked along the beach for a short distance and then waded into the lagoon. Wish I hadn't lost my fins and facemask, she thought. A gold butterfly fish fluttered past her feet. A blue fish, as long as her arm, swam slowly by. Then something bumped into her back.

She wheeled around, pulling the knife strapped to her calf. Red!

Again the colt, standing belly-deep in the water, bumped Jill with his small head. She sighed with relief and sheathed her knife. Puzzled, she splashed toward the beach with the colt following.

As she sat in the shallow water, the colt, shivering, bumped her arm again. Only when she moved up to the dry sand did he seem to relax, lying beside her more like a puppy than an orphaned mystery.

Jill frowned at him. "What were you trying to do? You scared me! I thought you were a shark or something. Sometimes sharks bump people before they taste them. Of course sharks big enough to bump into my back aren't usually in knee-deep water—"

At the tone of her voice, the colt backed up and stood facing her, switching his short broom-tail back and forth.

"Okay, okay," she said, relenting. "But why didn't you want me in the lagoon?" As she spoke, Jill kicked the water with her feet, and the colt shied away from her.

"Oh, you're afraid of water?"

The colt watched her, but he did not move closer.

"Come on. We'll talk about this after you eat."

The colt followed her to the tent, where she filled his makeshift bottle with evaporated milk. Head tilted back, he gurgled it down.

She broke off the large outer husk of a coconut and cracked the hard shell against a rock. After draining the milk, she cut out the meat and chopped it into small pieces. She took a handful and headed back to the lagoon, the colt tagging along behind.

"I want to teach you a thing or two about water." She put one foot in the water and offered him a piece of coconut.

"You know you like it," she urged. The colt wavered, then leaned forward to nibble the treat without wetting his hooves.

"Think you're smart, don't you." Jill stepped back.

This time the colt had to step into the water. He hesitated, then took the sweetmeat and nudged Jill for more.

"Come get it."

Once the colt had all four hooves in the water, he seemed to forget his fear.

"You see," Jill said, "you can't quit just because something looks tough." She scratched between the colt's ears and thumped him on the back.

While the colt meandered along the beach, poking his nose here and there, Jill knotted some rope and made him a halter. Finally, when the position of the sun and her stomach told her it was past noon, she saw her parents step from the platform of the sailboat into the dinghy. They revved the engine and headed toward the beach.

Jill helped pull the dinghy onto the beach. "Mom, did you find your log?"

Her mother shook her head. "No, but your father has the engine running smoothly again."

Uh-oh—I know what that means, Jill thought. She looked at Red, who was frisking on the beach. He's so beautiful and so much fun.

"We need to talk," her father said.

Jill bit her lip to keep from saying anything.

"We understand how you feel about the colt," he said gently. "I don't have an easy answer for this dilemma."

She followed her parents as they walked up the slope toward the campsite. Silently, they helped her strike the tent and pack the supplies in the dinghy.

Jill scooped up the coconut cubes that she had left to dry, then tossed them aside. Probably wouldn't need them, anyway.

And where's my knife? she thought. I know I left it here after I cut up the coconut. It's not important, compared to everything else. And yet—

"Mom," she said, "my knife is missing."

"That seems to be the way things have gone, doesn't it?"

Jill said nothing more. Maybe I was too distracted with the colt to pick it up, she thought. But she had the uneasy feeling that there was a reason for the missing knife—and the missing record book—and the shadow she had seen on the ledge.

"Jill," her father finally said, "we've considered your attachment to this colt from every angle. We don't have a practical solution. Remember, we're not here on vacation. Your mother has to finish her research and get back in a reasonable amount of time."

"I could take care of him until he's old enough to make it on his own," Jill said.

"This island looks like a rock fortress with only a few scrawny palm trees. Besides, how long could you live on coconuts?" her mother asked. "Coconut omelets, coconut tacos, spaghetti and coconuts—"

I know Mom's trying to make me smile, trying to make me feel better, but it won't work, Jill thought.

"It's not funny," she said.

"You're right. It's not." Her mother paused. "I'm sorry. Jill, we're miserable too. We love you, and we don't like to see you unhappy."

"Maybe we could bring him with us." Jill knew her suggestion was wildly impractical.

"He's not a puppy," her mother said. "You can't put him in a box or on a leash."

"And," her father asked, "how long would it take him to kick the cabin apart? Not to mention the onboard adjustments we would have to make. Just how big would the litter box have to be?"

"I thought about all that," Jill said, trying to hide her misery. "Is there any way we could take him to an island where there's grass? We can't let him starve. And he's alone!"

"I don't know." Her mother gestured helplessly. "I've studied marine life, but I don't know anything about horses."

"Look," her father said, "there just aren't any good options. He obviously doesn't belong here, and he obviously doesn't belong with us."

Jill took a deep breath. "Could we pray about it? Remember what you said? That God cares about everything in our lives. That He even knows how many hairs we have on our head. And," she said as an afterthought, "we need to pray about Mom's logbook too."

"Of course we should pray, Jill."

They sat down in the shade of the rocky mountain cliff. Jill pulled her Bible from her daypack, and her father took his large black Bible from a waterproof case.

"Well, we don't know what to do," he said, "so we'll ask for wisdom. James, chapter one. Jill, would you read?"

She nodded. Her throat hurt, but she was determined not to cry. She opened her Bible and read, *If any of you lack wisdom, let him ask of God . . .*

They held hands, and Jill prayed, "Lord, thank You for keeping us safe. You know I feel responsible for this colt I found, and I don't know what to do. Please give us wisdom. Thank You for caring about every area of our lives. And, God, You know how much work Mom has done. Please help her find her records. In Jesus' name—"

She clapped a hand over her mouth.

"What is it?" her mother asked.

"Mom, we didn't finish!"

"Finish what?"

"Looking at this place, this rock-island place!"

Her father nodded. "With all that's been going on, we've only checked out what we could reach on foot!"

Jill laughed with relief. Maybe the answer to the colt problem was on the other side of the mountains. If nothing else, she had a little more time to enjoy him.

Her father smiled at her. "We may find the solution yet. Guess we didn't need to pray after all, did we?"

She rolled her eyes. "Dad, you can't fool me."

"What, Jill?"

"When you pray and coincidences happen, you always tell that story."

He threw up his hands in feigned ignorance. "Story?"

"The one about the man falling off the roof who prays. Then his overalls catch on a nail, and he says, 'Never mind, God, I'm okay now.' "

"Point made," he said, laughing.

"So, could we bring Red onboard? Just until tomorrow. Just until we see what's on the rest of the island. Or until we find a place with fresh water and grass."

"We can't have a horse running around the boat," her father said.

"He sleeps most of the time," she said slowly.

"He could destroy thousands of dollars of equipment if he becomes frightened or gets loose."

"I'll make a pen, a horse pen, a—a paddock!"

He raised an eyebrow. "Where?"

"In my room."

"Jill, he's a horse!"

"He's just a small one," she whispered.

"He will do horse things on the boat."

"I'll take care of it."

Her father shook his head. "When Chip was a puppy, you made the same promise. Who took care of the dog things he did in the house?"

"I know." Jill had to look away. "I understand."

He paused, a thoughtful expression on his face. "Of course, you have matured. You have been very responsible—"

"Dad?"

"Just until we find an island with enough grass and water for—"

She threw her arms around his neck. "Thank you!"

She jerked back at the sound of a loud squeal. The colt! "Always into trouble!" she muttered, scrambling across the rocks. She took off running toward him.

A spear flashed in front of her, and she froze.

Unordered Accessories

CHAPTER 12

Jill screamed. Thrashing at her feet, its head impaled on a spear, was a snake. A long snake.

Her mother yanked her back against the cliff wall. Her father glanced up at a rocky ledge above their heads. "Well, one question is answered," he said grimly. "We're not the only ones here."

Jill threw her arms around the colt. They were both shaking. "Dad, what did he throw that spear at?"

"Let's hope the snake was the target—but we don't know."

She glanced at the snake, then quickly looked away. It was still writhing, and the dark sand glistened with its blood.

She remembered the falling rock, the shadow on the ledge, and her missing knife. She looked up at the ledge. The lava wall was pockmarked with holes and crevices, but not all of them looked natural. Clearly, someone had used a tool to chip footholds in the cliff wall.

"Dad—" She pointed to a man-made toehold.

"Good observation. Stay here."

"Rick, be careful," her mother whispered as he began to scale the wall.

He reached the ledge and swung up onto it. "No one here now. Anne, you and Jill get in the dinghy."

"The colt too—Dad said," Jill whispered to her mother.

"Jill, our lives may be in danger."

"I understand, Mom. Really, I do. I just want to take him where there's grass."

"If you can keep him calm, we'll try. If he causes a problem, even one time—"

"What's the holdup?" Her father shouted. "Go!"

They ran to the dinghy, the colt trotting close behind, and pushed the boat into the surf. Quickly, her father climbed back down the rock face and joined them.

"I didn't see anybody," he said.

Jill sat in the bottom of the dinghy and pulled the colt down beside her. She sighed with relief when the engine started. "What was it, Mom?"

"The spear or the snake?"

"The snake. What kind?"

"Sea snake."

"But I thought they lived in the water."

"They do. But sea snakes, *Hydrophidae*, give birth to live young. Most come ashore when they do."

"They're all poisonous, aren't they?"

"To different degrees, yes."

"Then whoever threw the spear—was it to hurt us or scare us or help us?" Jill asked.

"We may never know," her father said. "Maybe it was a little of each. I found out something, though."

"What?" Jill's mother asked.

"Whoever was on that ledge could easily observe us. And another thing, once you're on that ledge, you can see a crevice in the rock—big enough for a man to walk through."

"Then we were in danger and didn't even know it," said Jill. "Do you think the person who threw the spear stole my knife?"

He shrugged. "I don't know."

When they reached the *Sailfish*, Jill hurried up the ladder, then looked back over her shoulder. "You're not going to believe this!"

"What?" her mother asked, stepping into the cockpit.

Jill pointed to a large basket that overflowed with pineapples, mangos, bananas, and breadfruit. The missing knife and logbook were beside the basket.

"My log!" her mother said, grabbing it. "Thank You, Lord!"

"Give me a hand here," her father said, holding the colt in his arms. Jill helped pull Red into the cockpit.

Her father rubbed the stubble on his chin and stared at the basket. "Strange. Very strange, but it sure beats being hit with a spear." He picked up a mango. "It's safe to assume that an island that produces these would grow enough grass to feed a horse."

He turned to Jill. "But first things first. If you're going to keep this colt for a day or so, get him penned up and find some cat litter—some dry seaweed—something."

"Dad, I won't let you down."

"I don't want to see him loose. Not once."

A little later, Jill showed her father how she had provided for the colt. Confined in a large equipment crate, he was sound asleep on her sleeping bag.

By the time she settled the colt, the brief tropical twilight had come and gone. The boat's lights flicked on, and Jill remembered that she had planned to check the forward anchor light. But when she removed the cover, a strange object about the size of a golf ball fell into her hand. I don't know what this is, she thought, but Dad probably will.

Her father was using the sextant to make star shots. She tapped him on the arm. "Dad, look at this. I took the housing off the forward anchor light to see why the bulb was blinking. Look what I found!"

She held out the object. Her father's face turned grim when he saw it. "It's an electronic homing device. It radiates signals almost continually. Where did you find it?"

"In the same housing with the anchor light—the one that is far forward."

"Did you notice anything else unusual about that light?"

"Yes," she said, remembering a difference that she had thought was unimportant. "The cover of the anchor light isn't metal like the others. It looks like plastic."

Her father rubbed his chin thoughtfully. "The plastic housing was put on the anchor light so that the signals this device sent out could travel without being weakened. We've been bugged. Someone with a sensitive radio receiver is tracking us."

"Then . . ." The truth of what he was saying slowly dawned on Jill. "Then, they know where we are!"

Like a cat-and-mouse game, she thought. When will they pounce? What have they been waiting for?

"What will you do with it?"

"We'll look it over, then file it in the South Pacific. And we'll check for other unordered accessories. Although I imagine this is it."

Together, they headed down the companionway into the cabin and sat at the table. They were joined by her mother who had been in the lab examining the golden strands of hair from the basket.

"Jill," she said, "you can rename the colt Moses."

"What do you mean, Mom?"

"The hair in the basket and the dried blood probably came from him."

Her father laid the small transmitter on the table. Her mother stared at it, then rubbed her forehead as if she had a headache.

This is proof, Jill thought. Proof that someone has tracked our every move, even though we changed our course.

"Somebody had to handmake the low-loss plastic housing to look just like the metal original," her father said, turning it over in his hand. "That took some time, know-how, and a good working knowledge of electronics."

A chill swept over Jill. "It must have been done at the shipyard in Sydney."

"That's the only time it could have been done," he agreed. "If you hadn't checked that bulb, we would never have known."

He removed five batteries from the transmitter, jiggled them in the palm of his hand, then replaced them. "Let's use this device as a decoy to make whoever's tracking us think we're still moored—while we sail off."

He folded his arms and stared thoughtfully at the cabin floor. "This is probably a waste of time, but I'm going to give the *Sailfish* a quick once-over before I tape the bug to a buoy and toss it overboard."

"Dad, can I go?"

He laughed. "You may if you can. We're not depth-diving, just scooting under the boat. So, use your mom's gear. C'mon."

Jill pulled on scuba gear, checked the regulator and buoyancy compensator, switched on her dive light, and dove facedown into the dark water.

She eased around the boat, close behind her father as he swam on the surface, then ducked her head and dove under the hull. They aimed their dive lights upward, crisscrossing the underside of the boat with beams of light.

Almost instantly, Jill's light illuminated what looked like a handful of clay wrapped around the depth indicator.

Her father grabbed her arm and pulled her back.

She froze, staring at the circle of light. Wires led from the clay to a timing mechanism secured with waterproof tape. Red zeros flashed off and on. Was it a bomb?

Her father pushed her back and swam closer. Zeros still flashed on the digital time display.

If this is a bomb and the timer reads zero, why hasn't it exploded? she wondered.

Her father ran his flashlight over the circuit, tracing the wiring. Why was he taking so long?

Finally, he cut a wire, and two red lights went out. He carefully pried the bomb and the timer loose.

No big bang! Jill realized that she'd been holding her breath. She kicked her fins until she was clear of the boat, then broke through the surface, breathing a prayer of thanks.

They stored the dive equipment, then she hugged her father until he laughingly protested. "Jill, I have one rib left that isn't cracked, and it's starting to bend."

She smiled, still feeling shaky, and released her grip.

She found her mother clearing the table. Jill's daypack in hand, she was filling it with items that Jill had left on the table: books, shells, boomerang, candy wrappers, and a hairbrush. Without a word, Jill's father laid the bomb components on the table.

"Rick?" Her mother dropped the daypack, spilling its contents across the table.

"Yes, it's a bomb. And, yes, it was set. It should have already detonated. We thank God that it didn't."

"Thank God you're both unharmed." She paused, then looked up at her husband. "This isn't a conventional bomb."

"Oh, it's unconventional, all right, and clearly assembled by someone who knew what he—or she—was doing."

"How do you know, Dad?"

"It was booby-trapped." He sat down at the table and flicked one of the wires. "The obvious arming circuit was fake. I had to trace the real arming system."

"If you had touched the fake disarm—?"

"It would have detonated."

Jill nodded slowly. "The two lights that went out?"

"Arming and timing."

"Rick, why would someone bother to deceptively wire a bomb?"

"It appears that someone—most likely whoever did this—knows I worked with explosives in the Navy."

"But why, Rick? Who wants us dead?"

Jill heard a footstep on the companionway and looked up. A blond man holding a short-barreled Uzi stepped into the cabin. He stared at Jill and her parents with ice-blue eyes. Shark-eyes. She recognized his sleeveless black shirt and faded jeans.

Jill's father stood up, placing himself between the gunman and his family. While the man's attention was on her father, Jill eased the components of the bomb off the table and rested one arm on the boomerang.

"Sit down!" the man ordered.

Her father cooperated, but Jill knew he was sizing up his opponent, watching for a chance to disarm him without risking their lives.

"You've boarded us illegally. That's piracy." In surprise, Jill heard her own voice, squeaky with tension.

The gun swiveled to point at Jill. The man's lip twisted upward, as if she were a pesky fly.

Shiny black shoes descended the companionway steps. They belonged to a man wearing a gray suit—a handsome man with silvery-gray hair. Have I seen him before? Jill wondered.

He looked at Jill, then acknowledged her parents with a curt nod. "Pirates?" he said coldly. "No, this is a business call. Your activities have become a nuisance to my company, and I've come to put a stop to it." Hands behind his back and stiffly erect, he paced between the galley and the navigation station. Jill no longer thought he looked handsome. He looked dangerous.

"What's this about? What do you mean by 'nuisance'?" her father asked. "We're a university research team, gathering oceano-graphic data."

The man's jaw tightened. Jill knew her dad was watching for an opportunity. Maybe flattery would give him just that. She was shaking inside, but she had to try.

"Pardon me, sir," she said, "but how did you even know we were here?"

The man smiled patronizingly. "You told us—when you asked for detailed charts of the islands in this part of the South Pacific."

"But we wrote only to the chandler, the person who commissioned the *Sailfish*," Jill's mother said.

"So you did," he said, "but I make it a point to know what goes on in my business."

"Who are you?" whispered Jill.

A hard look flashed across his face, and she saw him as a man who would take pleasure in cruelty. "Who I am is none of your business, but you may call me 'Captain Bligh.'"

Captain
Bligh

CHAPTER 13

Bligh surveyed them coldly, then glanced around the interior of the *Sailfish*. "Yes, I'm president of the board of directors and owner of the company that commissioned this little yacht." He smoothed his silver hair with a well-manicured hand. "And a nice job we did. Too bad. A waste."

"Look, Bligh," her father began.

"Captain Bligh," the man said, as if correcting a child.

"Captain Bligh, I don't know who you think we are, but we are here to find islands away from polluted, heavily-fished areas that could be used as experimental nesting areas for endangered species of sea turtles."

Bligh laughed. "Sea turtles! Of course, the code name for your operation is Turtle. Tell me—how did you discover our dumping operation? Who else is involved? Who do you report to?"

"We are with a university research team—"

"Yes, yes, yes, so you told me. Maurice Richard Wyman, United States Naval officer, explosives expert! Enough lies!"

Jill caught her breath.

"This is a civilian mission," her father repeated. "We would never bring our daughter on a military operation."

At these words, the muscular man with the Uzi raised an eyebrow, looked at Bligh, and twisted one side of his face in a sardonic grin.

"In many countries," Bligh said, "there are children eight, nine years of age who are guerilla-warfare veterans."

"We don't do that in our country," her father said. "We don't send children to fight our wars—"

"Lies!" Bligh shouted. "No more lies, Wyman!"

Jill's mother spoke in a reasonable voice. "Captain, how could our operation here be a threat to you?"

"Don't insult my intelligence," he said. "We know where you're headed. Why else would you stop at the same islands that I marked as garbage dumps for radioactive waste?"

Her mother gasped, and Jill knew what she was thinking. Such an operation would endanger all life in the area.

"Your being here threatens my business." Bligh lowered his voice. "So—you meet with an unfortunate accident. Don't look so surprised. I gave you two warnings. You ignored them."

"Two warnings?" her father asked. "Don't you mean two murder attempts?"

The captain shrugged. "Whatever. If you'd run out of fuel as I planned, we would've been finished here long before you arrived. If, of course, you arrived at all."

"Then you planted the bomb?"

"Ah, yes, the bomb we planted when you docked in Suva." Bligh shook his head and frowned. "The transmitter kept sending signals that should've stopped when the bomb exploded." He raised one eyebrow. "For a professor, isn't disarming bombs an unusual hobby?"

Jill's father began to speak, but Bligh interrupted him. "Enough talk." He looked at his watch. "We'll tie you up, set an explosive charge with a time fuse, then leave. You will vanish at sea, and unfortunately, so will this fine yacht."

Bligh gave the gunman a command in a language that Jill didn't recognize.

Then the moment came that she had been praying for, but it came so swiftly that she had no time to think and barely time to react.

A noisy clatter on deck was followed by two loud splashes. In that distracting second, Jill grabbed the boomerang and slung it at the Uzi as hard as she could.

It missed. It struck the blond man on his kneecap instead. Jill ducked under the table, expecting a volley of bullets.

In the next moment she heard an odd noise in her cabin as if . . . Oh! That loose hinge on the crate!

A thud. A frightened squeal. Then a small fireball bolted through the room and ran headlong into the gunman.

The man hit his head on the edge of the navigation desk and fell to the floor. The Uzi discharged a short burst of fire. The lights went out.

Blindly Jill groped for the weapon. It had to be somewhere near the companionway. As her fingers touched the cold barrel, she heard the click of a gun being cocked.

A flashlight with a red lens cover illuminated the cabin. "You move—you die." She looked into the barrel of a gun.

She eased her hand away from the Uzi.

Oh, Red, wherever you are, stay out of here, she thought. He'd kill you in an instant. The gunman lay still, but Bligh was in control. He stepped back until he had all three of them in view. His sleeve was torn, and hatred contorted his features. He pulled out a handkerchief and mopped his forehead.

"Zagros! Tallish!" he barked, apparently calling for more men. He gave another order in a foreign language and stood on the steps, still holding the gun.

As if in response to his summons, the darkness of the night behind Bligh took shape.

Jill blinked as black shadows merged to form a man, sparsely clad, holding a spear. He struck the captain between the shoulders with the blunt end of the spear. Bligh sprawled on his face, and his handgun slid across the floor.

Jill grabbed for the gun. But this time there was no need to hurry.

The man had hit the floor in a belly slam. While he was still trying to get his breath, her father leaped to his side and tied his hands behind his back. Then he tied up the unconscious gunman.

"Keep an eye on these men," he said to Jill's mother. He handed her the Uzi and ammunition belt, and she pulled the slide back to reload.

Now Jill had time to wonder what had happened on deck. From the captain's shouted commands, he must have brought reinforcements. "Mom, did you see—?"

"No! I have no idea what that was."

"It looked like—like a cannibal!"

Her mother laughed and gave her a big hug. "If so, we'll give him our heartfelt thanks and invite him to dinner!"

Before going on deck, however, her father made a high-frequency radio transmission. It sounded to Jill like a message about weather, except none of the conditions in the message existed. She raised an inquiring eyebrow when he finished.

"Every seventh word stood for a coded message," he explained briefly. "I asked for a backup. Not that my team needs it!"

I hope that backup comes soon, Jill thought.

Her father put a hand on her shoulder. "Jill, you really took a risk," he said. "I'm glad you chose your words carefully."

"I was scared to death. And I thought you might tell me to be quiet."

Her mother smiled. "Why would we do that? We expect you to use good judgment, and you did."

While her mother guarded the prisoners, Jill took the handgun and stood watch at the cabin entrance.

Her father checked the radar. "It's clear that Bligh boarded with a small party," he said, "but we don't know what happened to the others who were with him. We only know they didn't answer his commands. If they came by raft, their boat should be nearby."

He pointed to the radar screen. "And there it is, about two miles south. I want to find out what happened to his men."

Now that the intruders were tied up, Jill went looking for the colt. She found him in the galley, where he had pushed a plastic jar into a corner. He looked up, his nose streaked with jelly.

He stepped toward her, unsure of his footing on the rocking boat, and pushed his warm, fluttering nose against her shirt, snuffing at her pockets and smearing her clothes.

She scolded him halfheartedly, then led him back to the crate. The side she had hinged hung loose, so she nailed it shut.

Her father poked his head through the doorway. "When this all started, what exactly did you see?"

"Someone knocked Bligh down—with a pole or spear or something. I'll bet it was the same person who killed that snake."

"Let's go see." Her father held the gun ready and preceded Jill up the companionway. Would the rest of Bligh's men be waiting on deck to ambush them? she wondered.

Two drenched seamen sat huddled and shivering in the cockpit. Standing over them was a wild-looking man, tall and fierce, holding a wooden spear as if it were a club. Dark as the shadows around him, he was covered with tattoos and clothed only in a loincloth. He stood at ease on the rolling deck as if he were part of the very ocean from which he had mysteriously appeared.

Jill stared. "Are you a cannibal?" She said it without thinking and then wished she hadn't.

"I prefer hamburger and fries," the man said. Before Jill could recover from her astonishment, he announced, "I am Tevake." He lifted his spear. "And this I have named the Sword of the Spirit. Very quickly it made believers of these two doubters, convicting them of their sin, righteousness, and judgment to come."

The two men on either side of him rubbed their heads and moaned.

"Mr. Tevake, I'm Jill." She stepped forward. "This is my dad, Rick Wyman."

Her father cleared his throat. "We're grateful for your help," he said, shaking Tevake's hand. "But how did you know we needed it?"

"These men," Tevake said, "like to play with explosives. They have made big changes in Red Horse Island. Changes which have not improved the value of the real estate."

"What do you mean?" she asked.

"For some reason that I do not understand, they used explosives to make a tunnel. Their explosions weakened the foundation of the mountain. Heavy rains and a mudslide caused the death of several horses. They came in a large ship. Since they left, I have watched every day for their return."

"We have a good idea what they were up to," her father said. "Apparently they planned to store radioactive waste—to use this island as a nuclear waste garbage dump."

"So . . . " Tevake said. "*Mais oui!* The tunnel gave them access to the valley, a good hiding place for their illegal cargo."

Her father nodded. "Behind these cliffs, their activity would be well-hidden from the authorities."

"If they went to all that trouble, they must have planned to use this place again and again," Jill said.

"That would explain many things," Tevake said.

He inclined his head courteously toward them. "I have been slow in welcoming you. I thought you might be with those men—until I saw you with the Book of Life."

What did he mean?

"You read from a book like the one my granddaughter gave me." Tevake pulled a small black book from his pouch.

A New Testament. "You're a Christian!" Jill exclaimed.

"Yes," he replied, "and I recognized that you, also, are followers of Jesus."

"Well, God's ways are mysterious," her father said slowly. "This is remarkable." His gaze swept the deck, and then it sharpened. "Jill, these men still look a little dazed. Check the locker for rope. Tie their hands and feet. We'll add these two pirates to your mother's collection."

"Rick, is everything all right?" her mother called from below. "Who are you talking to?"

"A friend," he replied. "And yes, everything is fine—I think." He conferred with Tevake. "We've located the ship these men came from. If they don't return soon, I expect more trouble."

"You may count on me," Tevake said gravely.

"We have no weapons except Bligh's," Jill's father said. "And his explosives won't even dent a steel-hulled ship."

An idea was taking shape in Jill's mind. "I've been studying World War II, and—Dad, wasn't the *Bismarck* disabled because a torpedo hit the rudder?" She paused to think it through. "Do we have enough explosives to damage their steering system?"

"It's worth a try," said her father. He glanced at Tevake. "No telling how many men he's got over there. Okay, we'll use Bligh's explosives to disable the rudder, and they won't be able to steer."

Tevake raised his spear in agreement.

"Let's use Bligh's raft too—it's bigger than ours," her father said. He and Tevake loaded the scuba gear, then he went below to discuss the plan with her mother. Jill trailed along behind, hoping he'd ask her to come too.

"It's risky," her father was saying, "but I need Jill's help. I'm not quite sure about that old man—not yet."

Her mother nodded from where she sat with one hand on the Uzi. "You've been very responsible, Jill," she said. "Don't take any unnecessary chances. I'll be praying for you all."

Minutes later, they set off. The night was overcast and the air chilly. Jill zipped up her jacket and strained to see across the dim expanse of water. Was anyone coming? Surely someone would hear the roar of their outboard motor and try to ambush them.

She glanced at Tevake. He stared silently ahead, his dark face alert, and she knew he'd see or hear anything long before they did.

When the shadowy superstructure of the freighter appeared, her father turned off the engine.

No anchor lights lit the bow and stern. No voices broke the stillness. The ship appeared to be deserted.

They paddled closer. An armed guard leaned against the rail, but they floated silently past him. The man made no sound to indicate that he saw the raft or its occupants.

Jill tied the raft to an old chainlink anchor. Her father pulled on his fins and slipped the mask over his head, then she helped him with the tank harness. He checked his breathing regulator, patted Jill on the shoulder, and eased into the water.

Seconds later, she saw his dive light switch on, so she turned to Tevake. The old Polynesian had disappeared. Had he led them into a trap?

A moving shadow above caught her attention. Tevake, spear slung across his back, was climbing the anchor chain.

Maybe I should follow him, she thought. What is he up to? Anyway, I can't stand guard for Dad down here. I need to be higher—where I can see. I need to make sure he isn't caught while he sets the charge.

She grabbed the chain and climbed slowly up the large links. It was far more difficult than it looked. Partway up, she stopped to catch her breath and glanced down at the raft. Dizzy! She closed her eyes for a minute.

After that, she kept her eyes fixed on the place where the chain disappeared into the hawsehole, and she climbed as fast as she could. Soon her hands were slippery with sweat.

When she finally reached the rail, she rubbed her hands on her jeans one at a time, then she leaned against the ship to wait.

She tried to ignore her thudding heart and closed her eyes to picture what her father would be doing at that moment. First, he'd have to swim under the stern, then he'd shine his hooded light on the rudderstock to check it out. He'd probably have to use his knife to scrape off barnacles. Somewhere between the water level and the rudder crosshead, he would set the charge Captain Bligh had meant for the *Sailfish*.

The seconds dragged by as she waited for him to signal that he had resurfaced. The night chill crept under her jacket. Finally, she climbed on deck to look for Tevake. No surprise that the agile old man was long gone.

Footsteps approached, and she heard muffled voices. Quickly she hid behind a large wooden crate that smelled like diesel oil.

Two men were mumbling to each other, and one of them was humming. "Give me that. You've 'ad enough." His speech was slurred, and she figured they'd both probably had enough of whatever they were arguing over.

The voices drew nearer, and she crouched lower behind the crate. She was edging back against the rail when she bumped into something. A human leg? She looked up.

A huge sailor towered over her. "Well, what 'ave we 'ere!" he cried, and a rough hand grabbed her by the ear.

Touch
a Star

CHAPTER 14

The bearded sailor pulled Jill so close that she could smell his foul breath. Her ear burned, and she squirmed, trying to escape. The other man's muscular forearm went under her chin, squeezing her in a headlock, and she closed her eyes.

"'Ow nice, a bit o' entertainment!" he said, and both men laughed as she struggled, gasping for breath.

The man tightened his grip around her neck, and she began to choke. But suddenly he yelled and released her. Jill opened her eyes to see Tevake leaping to the deck. His spear flashing in the darkness, he looked as fierce as an avenging angel.

She pulled free of her startled captors and scrambled over the rail. As she climbed down the anchor chain, she heard a familiar sound. Two loud thumps—*whap! whop!* Then a shadow plunged over the rail of the ship and disappeared into the black waves below her.

Her father was waiting in the raft, and he helped her climb down from the chain. Tevake surfaced nearby. The engine coughed, stalled for an endless moment, then started.

Above them were the sounds of running feet and angry shouts. Bullets zinged past, speeding their hasty takeoff. Her father gunned the engine, and the raft jumped forward, almost throwing Jill backwards into the ocean. But after that, the raft skimmed the waves, leaving the freighter far behind.

They had just boarded the *Sailfish* when the world seemed to rock with an explosion. The deck shook beneath her feet. A burst of flame lit the sky, briefly illuminating the freighter. Then all was dark on the horizon.

Jill caught her breath. "Dad! Their running lights are on!" The ship's engines rumbled, and the lights seemed to grow brighter, as if the huge vessel were bearing down on them. "But look . . ." She jumped to her feet.

The freighter was turning in circles.

"Yow!" her father shouted. "She's not answering her helm! David, one. Goliath, zero!"

"Dad, you did it! You did it!"

Her father laughed. "Our best, working together—and God did the rest."

He slapped Tevake on the back and thanked him again. Then he said, "Jill, brilliant military strategy. Good thing you remembered the *Bismarck*."

After they'd finished unloading the raft, Jill had to ask the questions that still bothered her.

"Mr. Tevake, did you—" She stopped, embarrassed to inquire about her knife.

"Did I take the book and the knife?"

She nodded.

"Yes," he said quietly. "I was watching for the others when you came. I thought the words and numbers that were written in the book might tell why those men—and you—came to Red Horse Island."

"But then you brought our things back?"

"*Mais oui*. When I saw that you looked to God and to the Bible for wisdom, I knew that you intended no harm."

"And you're the one who killed the sea snake?"

"The snake, *oui*. A very poisonous snake."

"We have much to thank you for, Tevake," her father said. "Come, I want you to meet my wife."

Jill's mother shook Tevake's hand and thanked him several times. "Please sit down," she said. "You must be thirsty."

After checking on the prisoners, her father joined them.

Her mother handed glasses of iced tea around. "You're the only person on this island?" she asked Tevake. "How did that come about?"

"I was caught in a storm—just as you were," he said, and Jill wondered about the story behind those simple words.

"What will you do now?" she asked.

"I have repairs to finish on my boat, then I will go to Tahiti." He paused. "To see my granddaughter."

Jill had only one question left, but she dreaded asking it. "Sir, we, I—found this colt, and—well, we didn't see any fresh water or grass, so we didn't know where he came from or where to take him."

"Things are not always as they seem," Tevake said.

Jill looked at him in surprise. "Then . . . ?"

Tevake told them how he had come ashore after a storm had driven him off course and damaged his boat, and he too had thought the island was a barren, rocky place. Then he had discovered its fertile, wooded valleys and clear springs. "For many years I had heard of a place called Red Horse Island, and I thought it was just a legend. But the horses are as real as the colt you found."

"And yet you have decided to leave," said Jill's mother softly.

The old man smiled. "When I came here, driven by the storm, I was running away. I thought I had nothing to live for. Alone in this quiet place, I began to read the Book, a gift from my granddaughter. Now I will return and tell her that I have many reasons to live. God loves me, and He has forgiven me because of Jesus Christ. I will not be careless with my life anymore because I belong to God."

Why would an adult want to run away? Jill wondered. What had happened that made him want to leave his family? Not knowing what to say, she just nodded.

"So the colt belongs on the island?" she asked.

He gestured toward the mountains. "Beyond the cliffs—a beautiful valley."

"And you would—take him back for us?"

He nodded, as if he understood her reluctance.

"I'll get him," she said.

She hurried to her cabin and pried the crate open. She put her arms around the colt's warm neck and buried her head in the soft, fuzzy hair. Then she released him and began to scratch between his ears. For the first time, she noticed the faint outline of a star on his forehead. It was just a shade paler than his bright copper coat.

She gently traced the star. "I'm sad you have to go, but I'm not sorry we met."

Red switched his tail and pushed against her, looking for sugar. She laughed and hugged him again.

After she and her father had managed to get the colt up on deck, her father turned to Tevake. "I've made radio contact with the U.S. Navy so our prisoners can be picked up. The commander said he'll provide you with passage home."

Tevake gestured toward the ocean. "For many years before I left to study at the university, this was my life. When I am ready, I will return to Tahiti."

A few minutes later, he and the colt boarded the outrigger canoe, and Jill watched sadly as Tevake paddled toward the dark island. Would she ever see them again?

The rumble of a helicopter jerked her attention to the sky, and soon the aircraft hovered over the *Sailfish*. A spotlight illuminated the entire sailboat.

"Hello down there!" came a deep voice from a bullhorn. "This is Commander Fessenden of the United States Navy. Don't get underway. We're coming aboard."

A rope dropped to the afterdeck, and three figures in Navy camouflage slid down. The commander surveyed the situation and laughed, slapping Jill's father on the back. Apparently, they had been former classmates at Annapolis.

"I like the signal flare you sent up," he said. "We were trying to pin down your exact location when we saw the explosion. Now that just beats all. Here we've been chasing those men around the Pacific for the last two weeks, and you have them hog-tied and gift-wrapped for us. We'll take custody of the prisoners and the crew of that freighter you disabled."

"Who are these men, anyway?" her mother asked.

"Mercenaries. His crew is made up of mercenaries. They're from different countries, hired to do whatever dirty job Bligh digs up."

"Then who *is* Bligh?" Jill asked.

"He's the son of an American expatriate," Fessenden replied. "When he was fourteen years old, his father died and he immigrated to the States with his maternal grandparents who settled in Akron, Ohio. His grandfather opened a shoe store there. Guess he thought he'd never be well-heeled if he followed in his granddad's footsteps. Heh, heh! Oh, yes, one more thing, Captain Bligh's real name is Saul Marcos."

The men that Jill knew only as Bligh, Zagros, Tallish, and Shark-Eyes were hoisted aboard the helicopter, arguing in a foreign language.

After the last prisoner had been transferred, one of the sailors turned to Commander Fessenden. "Sir, I know a little of their language. They're saying they were attacked by a small red horse and a tall wild man."

The commander grinned. "Rick, would you know what they're talking about?"

Her father laughed. "You've got to remember, they've had a rough night."

Fessenden nodded, apparently satisfied with the evasive answer. "Well, what now?" he asked. "You and your family have solved an important case for the United States Navy. Will you head back home?"

"After we've finished our research, we will," her mother said. "But I must admit, the rest of our trip will be anticlimactic."

Jill's father and the commander talked for a few more minutes, promising to meet again and discuss old times, and then the Navy men were hoisted back into the waiting helicopter.

After the twinkling lights of the helicopter vanished, Jill stood on deck for a long time. She gazed at the island they would soon leave. From what Tevake had said, it must be beautiful. Lush valleys . . . silver waterfalls . . . hidden caves. And animals. Wild horses, a mischievous pig—and the colt!

DANGER FOLLOWS

Her mother placed a hand on her shoulder. "Penny for your thoughts."

"They're worth lots more than that," Jill said wistfully. "On our way back to Australia, could we stop and see how Red is doing?"

Her mother smiled and hugged her. "We'll see, Jill. We'll see."